可以馬上學會的

超強英語閱讀課

最有效率的閱讀訓練法
破解閱讀密碼、突破瓶頸

一次搞定：TOEIC · TOEFL · IELTS · 英檢 · 學測 · 會考

附 MP3

蘇盈盈 · 珊朵拉 ── 合著

BOOK HOUSE
布可屋

最有效率的聽力訓練法
破解閱讀密碼、突破瓶頸

　　隨著國際化的快速趨勢，為了跟上潮流，學好國際第一通用外語－英語，就是大家眼前最重要的功課。學英語的好處很多：除了可以開拓自己的眼界、結交更多朋友、獲得多元的第一手消息、瀏覽網站更方便等，影響我們最大的，無非是精通英語在職場上佔盡的優勢！想進國際化的大公司，不會英語那就真是 No way 了！

　　學語言，除了希望可以閱讀、欣賞他國文化外，最希望的當然還是能說出流利道地的外文，跟外國人輕鬆溝通囉！為了讓讀者有更親切的學習環境，本公司特別編撰「超強英語」系列，強力增進您的英語能力。書加 MP3 雙管齊下，讓您彈指翻閱之間，英語實力馬上提升；加上 MP3 的強力放送，讓自己無時不泡「英語澡」，保證流利英語迅速脫口說！

　　本書是一本能有效提升閱讀能力的優良書籍，特別編排了多種不同的情境及文體－如電子郵件、一般郵件、生活會話、敘述文、報紙、食譜等。讓您跟著書中人物，麗迪亞、艾瑞克、喬治姨丈……一起體驗美國風情，並快速飆高英語實力！內容活潑有趣，除了可以當作英語的寫作範本外，更可運用於日常生活中。每篇課文後，都有實用字彙及句型補充，句型片語更附上英文說明，提供讀者更貼近原意的詮釋，使用句型更能得心應手！課文與單字句型都熟讀後，再來是閱讀測驗，讓您馬上評分，學習效果看得見！

隨著英語教材日漸生活化的趨勢，英語閱讀亦應打破傳統制式的學習法，以更符合時代需要的技巧來學習。想要有效提升自我英語實力，聽、說、讀、寫全方位加強，本書絕對是你不可或缺的好幫手。除了實質上提升閱讀能力外，更具備了趣味性及實用性，能激發讀者自動自發的學習心，達到事半功倍的成果，聽讀激增 100 分。本書由專業英語作家精心撰寫，道地且精彩，讀來趣味橫生。全書三十三單元的流暢文章，由美國人來帶您進入英語閱讀的新境界，跟著作者的精心安排，按部就班學習，英語能力迅速精進。每單元都包括以下四個學習重點：

Reading: 課文內容相當生活化，除了可增進讀者閱讀能力外，更可將文中所學的單字、對話運用到生活上，讓您快速提升英語會話能力。

Vocabulary: 搭配簡潔中譯，重點單字一口氣學會，閱讀文章更加輕鬆迅速。

Useful Sentences: 從課文精選出來的實用句型，輔以英文解釋及範例對話，讓您能深入了解，實地運用。

Review Questions: 閱讀測驗讓您驗收成果，並可提升您整理重點的能力。

本書內容涵蓋實用文章、書信往來、一般會話、報章雜誌報導等，係針對欲提升其閱讀能力，及學習英語實用生活會話的讀者。內文及測驗考題均附有中文翻譯，方便讀者參考對照。內容深入淺出，

是一般英語學習者自修的最佳選擇，也是學生精進英文能力的好幫手。

隨書附贈光碟，實況模擬，專業錄音，搭配學習，效果加倍！

本系列最大特色：

1. **原汁原味‧美語文章：** 為呈現原汁原味的美語文章，特聘請英語教材專家撰寫，內容專業、流暢，用字精練，言簡易賅，看完馬上實力突飛猛進！

2. **閱讀技巧‧一次學會：** 各類文體的閱讀訓練，勤加熟讀，英語閱讀能力瞬間大躍進。

3. **嚴謹編撰‧專業錄音：** 由美籍專業播音員，精心錄製的精質MP3，發音純正標準，腔調自然符合情境，讓您跟著道地流暢的語調，快速學會正確美式發音。

4. **精讀瀏覽‧同步提升：** 文體有長有短，涵蓋各式文章的精華，跟著作者精心設計的內容，按部就班學習，英語閱讀技巧即刻掌握。

按部就班跟著本書所設計的學程加以學習，您將迅速進入英語閱讀天地，快速破解英語閱讀密碼！

編者 謹識

CONTENTS

CONTENTS

CONTENTS

Chapter 4
Aunt June 茱兒阿姨

CONTENTS

Chapter 5
An End-of-Summer Barbecue 夏末 BBQ

Answers 解答

Chapter ❶ Meet Lydia!
遇見麗迪亞

Unit 1 Lydia's Email Account

June 5th,

Hey Kelly!

What's up? I arrived in the U.S. late last night, and I'm so tired! Why am I writing you this email then instead of sleeping? Well, that's because I have a bad case of jet lag!

So, until I feel as though I can sleep, let me spend a little time telling you about my trip. I was really sad at the airport when I said goodbye to my mom and my dad. I cried when they waved goodbye to me. But when I got on the plane, I felt better, because I knew that I was going to have a great summer studying English in America!

My aunt June and uncle George picked me up from the airport in L.A. My cousin couldn't come because he had a baseball practice to go to. I can hardly wait until I get to see him play. He's a pitcher, and he's supposed to be great! My aunt says that if I'm not too tired tomorrow, then we can all go to see a game together. Won't that be fun!

Well, I'm starting to feel sleepy now. So, I'll end this email here. Write back soon!

Your friend,
Lydia

麗迪亞的電子郵件

六月五日

嗨，凱莉，

妳好嗎？我昨晚很晚抵達美國，覺得累極了。但為什麼我卻在這兒寫電子郵件給妳，而不是去睡覺呢？唉，那是因為我有嚴重的時差！

所以，在我想睡覺之前，讓我花一點時間告訴你我的旅程吧。當我在機場跟我的爸媽道別時，我真的很難過。當他們對我揮手再見時，我哭了。但當我踏上飛機以後，我覺得好多了，因為我知道在美國學英文的這個夏天將會很棒。

我阿姨茱兒和姨丈喬治到洛杉磯的機場接我。我表哥沒有來，因為他得去練習棒球。我已經等不及要看他打球了。他是個投手，應該打得很棒。我阿姨說如果我不太累的話，明天我們就可以一起去看比賽。那一定相當有趣！

喔，我現在開始想睡了。所以我就寫到這兒了，要趕快回信給我喔！

妳的朋友

麗迪亞

email account	電子郵件信箱
jet lag	時差
wave	揮手
practice	練習
pitcher	棒球投手；投擲者
hardly	很難地；幾乎不

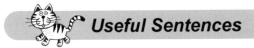

Useful Sentences

◎ Supposed to 想像的；假定、假設的

used to say that one should do something
用以說明某人應該做某事

A: Weren't you supposed to do your homework?
你不是應該做你的家庭作業嗎？

B: Yes, but I decided to watch TV instead.
是啊，但是我決定要看電視。

◎ Won't that be fun 一定很有趣

used to say that somebody thinks that something will be fun
用以表示某人認為某事一定很有趣

A: I'm going to Mary's party tomorrow!
我明天要去參加瑪麗的派對

B: Won't that be fun!
那一定很有趣！

Review Questions

1. Who is Lydia writing to?
   A) a friend   B) her teacher
   C) her mother   D) her brother

2. Why can't Lydia sleep?
   A) She is hungry.   B) She is worried.
   C) She has jet lag.   D) She is tired.

3. Why is Lydia in America?
   A) to sleep   B) to study
   C) to travel   D) to escape

4. Who picked Lydia up from the airport?
   A) her mom and dad   B) her cousin
   C) her aunt and uncle   D) her friend

5. What sport does Lydia's cousin play?
   A) baseball   B) soccer
   C) basketball   D) tennis

測驗題庫中譯

1. 麗迪亞在寫信給誰？

    A) 一個朋友   B) 她的老師

    C) 她的媽媽   D) 她的哥哥

2. 為什麼麗迪亞睡不著？

    A) 因為她很餓   B) 因為她很擔心

    C) 因為她有時差問題   D) 因為她很疲倦

3. 為什麼麗迪亞到美國去？

    A) 去睡覺   B) 去唸書

    C) 去旅遊   D) 去逃難

4. 誰到機場接麗迪亞呢？

    A) 她的媽媽和爸爸   B) 她的表哥

    C) 她的阿姨和姨丈   D) 她的朋友

5. 麗迪亞的表哥從事什麼運動？

    A) 棒球   B) 足球

    C) 籃球   D) 網球

Unit 2 Good Morning!

Lydia's uncle wakes Lydia up.

Uncle George : Good morning, Lydia!

Lydia : Good morning, Uncle George.

Uncle George : Did you sleep well?

Lydia : Not too bad! What time is it?

Uncle George : It's already eleven am.

Lydia : Oh! I didn't mean to sleep in so late!

Uncle George : That's OK! Traveling always wears me out, too. Are you hungry?

Lydia : Yes! Let me wash up, and then I'll come down to eat.

After Lydia washes up, she goes downstairs and finds her uncle cooking in the kitchen.

Lydia : So, what do you have for breakfast?

Uncle George : Breakfast?! You're too late for breakfast! I'm preparing lunch!

Lydia : OK, then. What's for lunch?

Uncle George : I'm making soup and sandwiches.

Lydia : Is there anything that I can do to help?

Uncle George : Sure there is! You can lend a hand by stirring the soup to make sure that it doesn't burn.

Lydia : Where are the spoons?

Uncle George : We keep them in the drawer next to the stove.

Uncle George is making sandwiches while Lydia looks after the soup.

Uncle George : What do you like on your sandwich?

Lydia : What have you got?

Uncle George : I have two kinds of meat: turkey and ham.

Lydia : I'd prefer turkey.

Uncle George : Turkey it is! Would you like tomatoes and lettuce?

Lydia : Yes, please. I'd like both.

Uncle George : How about mustard?

Lydia : No, thank you. I don't like mustard. But do you have any mayonnaise?

Uncle George : Yes, I do.

早安！

麗迪亞的姨丈把她叫醒。

喬治姨丈：早安，麗迪亞！

麗迪亞：　早安，喬治姨丈！

喬治姨丈：妳睡得好嗎？

麗迪亞：　還不錯。現在幾點了？

喬治姨丈：已經是上午十一點了。

麗迪亞：　喔，我不是故意睡這麼晚的！

喬治姨丈：沒關係，旅行也總是使我精疲力竭。妳餓了嗎？

麗迪亞：　是啊，讓我盥洗一下，然後我再下去吃東西。

麗迪亞盥洗完畢到樓下以後，看見姨丈正在廚房煮東西。

麗迪亞：　那麼，早餐吃什麼呢？

喬治姨丈：早餐？妳吃早餐已經太遲了。我正在做午餐。

麗迪亞：　喔，那午餐吃什麼？。

喬治姨丈：我在煮湯還有做三明治。

麗迪亞：　有什麼我可以幫得上忙的嗎？

喬治姨丈：當然有啦！妳可以幫忙攪拌湯以免燒焦。

麗迪亞：　湯匙在哪裡呢？

喬治姨丈：我們把湯匙放在火爐旁邊的抽屜裡。

麗迪亞在顧湯的時候，喬治姨丈則做著三明治。

喬治姨丈： 妳想要在三明治裡加些什麼？

麗迪亞： 你準備了什麼呢？

喬治姨丈： 我有兩種肉，火雞和火腿肉。

麗迪亞： 我要火雞肉。

喬治姨丈： 那就放火雞肉。妳要放蕃茄或者生菜嗎？

麗迪亞： 好啊，謝謝。我兩種都要。

喬治姨丈： 那芥茉呢？

麗迪亞： 不了，謝謝。我不喜歡芥茉。不過你有美乃滋嗎？

喬治姨丈： 有啊，我有。

Vocabulary

wake somebody up	把某人叫醒
stir	攪拌；搖動
spoon	湯匙
drawer	抽屜
stove	火爐
prefer	寧願；更喜歡
turkey	火雞；火雞肉

tomato	蕃茄
lettuce	生菜；萵苣
mustard	芥茉
mayonnaise	美乃滋

 **Useful Sentences**

◎ Lend a hand 伸出援手、幫忙

to help 幫忙

A: This box is so heavy!
這個箱子真重！

B: Wait! Let me lend a hand. If we both help to carry it, the job will be much easier!
等等！讓我幫忙吧！如果我們一起抬，事情就簡單多了！

◎ Look after something 照顧、照應某事物

to take responsibility for something
負起某事物的責任

A: I have to go to the store for a few minutes, but the baby is sleeping.

我得到商店去一趟，可是寶寶在睡覺。

B: Don't worry! I'll look after him while you're out.

別擔心，妳不在時我會照顧他的。

 Review Questions

1. Who wakes Lydia up?

   A) her friend   B) her uncle

   C) her aunt   D) her brother

2. What time is it when Lydia wakes up?

   A) eleven in the morning   B) twelve o'clock

   C) one in the afternoon   D) six at night

3. What is Lydia's uncle preparing in the kitchen?

   A) breakfast   B) lunch

   C) dinner   D) dessert

4. What can Lydia do to help?

   A) make the sandwiches   B) eat the turkey

   C) buy the food   D) stir the soup

5. What does Lydia not want on her sandwich?

   A) turkey   B) tomatoes

   C) mustard   D) mayonnaise

 測驗題庫中譯

1. 誰把麗迪亞叫醒的？

   A) 她的朋友   B) 她的姨丈

   C) 她的阿姨   D) 她的哥哥

2. 麗迪亞醒來時幾點了？

   A) 早上十一點   B) 十二點

   C) 下午一點鐘   D) 傍晚六點

3. 麗迪亞的姨丈在廚房準備什麼？

   A) 早餐   B) 午餐

   C) 晚餐   D) 點心

4. 麗迪亞可以幫什麼忙？

   A) 做三明治   B) 吃火雞肉

   C) 買食物   D) 攪拌湯汁

5. 麗迪亞不想要放什麼東西在她的三明治裡面？

   A) 火雞肉   B) 蕃茄

   C) 芥茉   D) 蛋黃醬

MP3-4

Unit 3 — Cleaning up

Lydia and her uncle have just finished eating their lunch.

Lydia : Mmm! That was delicious!

Uncle George : There's nothing like a nice hot bowl of soup, is there?

Lydia : Nope. I guess it's time to tidy up. What can I do to help?

Uncle George : You can clear the table. I'll put the leftover food away in the fridge. Then we can wash the dishes.

Lydia : That sounds like a plan!

Lydia has put the dirty dishes in the sink.

Lydia : I'll wash the dishes, if you like.

Uncle George : That would be great. And I'll dry them.

Lydia : Just one thing. Where do you keep the dish soap?

Uncle George : We keep the dish soap under the sink with the other cleaning supplies.

Lydia : In this cupboard?

Uncle George : No, the one to the left. See it?

Lydia : Yes, I do!

Lydia and her uncle have put the dishes away. The kitchen is clean.

Uncle George : So, what would you like to do for the rest of the afternoon?

Lydia : Well, I think I'd like to take it easy. I'm still pretty tired.

Uncle George : I have to go to the office this afternoon. But I will leave a set of keys to the house in case you want to go out for a walk.

Lydia : That's a good idea. Some fresh air might just do me good!

Uncle George : Speaking of walks, I know somebody who might like to take a walk with you.

Lydia : Who is that?

Uncle George : Our dog, Pepper! You haven't met her yet because she's out in the backyard. But allow me to introduce you two. Here, Pepper!

清理

麗迪亞和姨丈剛吃完他們的午餐。

麗迪亞： 嗯，真好吃！

喬治姨丈： 沒有什麼比的上一碗好喝的熱湯，是吧？

麗迪亞： 沒錯。我想是該收拾一下了。我可以幫什麼忙嗎？

喬治姨丈： 妳可以清理一下桌子，我把剩下的菜放進冰箱裡。
然後我們就可以洗碗了。

麗迪亞： 聽起來不錯。

麗迪亞已經把髒碗盤都放進洗碗槽裡了。

麗迪亞： 如果你不反對，我要幫忙洗碗。

喬治姨丈： 那就太好了。我來擦。

麗迪亞： 有一個問題，洗碗皂在哪裡？

喬治姨丈： 在洗碗槽下面，跟其他清洗用具放在一起。

麗迪亞： 在這個櫥櫃裡嗎？

喬治姨丈： 不是，是左邊那一個，妳看到了嗎？

麗迪亞： 嗯，我看到了。

麗迪亞和姨丈把碗盤都收拾好了，廚房已經清潔溜溜了。

喬治姨丈： 那麼，下午妳想做什麼呢？

麗迪亞： 嗯，我想要休息一下。我還是覺得很累。

喬治姨丈： 我下午得去上班。不過我會留一副家裡的鑰匙給你，以免得妳想要出去走走。

麗迪亞： 那真是個好主意。呼吸一點新鮮空氣對我應該很好。

喬治姨丈： 説到散步，我知道有人也許會想要跟妳出去走走。

麗迪亞： 誰啊？

喬治姨丈： 我們的狗，胡椒！妳還沒見過牠，因為牠在外頭的院子裡。請容許我介紹你們兩個認識。到這裡來，胡椒！

 *Vocabulary*

delicious	美味的；好吃的
bowl	碗
tidy up	清理乾淨
clear the table	把桌子清乾淨
leftover	剩下的
sink	水槽；碗槽
soap	肥皂
cupboard	櫥櫃
a set of something	一組物品

Useful Sentences

◎ Take it easy 放輕鬆、休息

to relax; to not work hard 放鬆；不太認真做事情

A: How was your vacation? Did you have a good time?
你的假期怎麼樣？玩得愉快嗎？

B: I did. I just went to the beach and took it easy.
很愉快。我到海邊去放鬆一下。

◎ Do somebody good 對…好

to be good for somebody 對於某人很好

A: I've been thinking of joining a gym.
我一直在考慮要不要加入健身俱樂部。

B: What a great idea! Some exercise would do you good.
很好的主意啊。做些運動對你很好。

◎ Speaking of … 說到

used to make a connection to a new idea based on something that was just said.

用以連接一個新的話題，此話題奠基於之前談過的話。

A: For my birthday, I got some new video games and a bike!
我生日時得到一個新的電玩遊戲和腳踏車。

B: Speaking of bikes, did you hear that Helen's got stolen?
說到腳踏車，妳聽說海倫的腳踏車被偷了嗎？

 **Review Questions**

1. What do Lydia and her uncle George do after lunch?

    A) They clean the kitchen.

    B) They go to the office.

    C) They go for a walk.

    D) They eat some sandwiches.

2. What does Lydia do first?

    A) She washes the dishes.

    B) She dries the dishes.

    C) She clears the table.

    D) She puts the leftovers in the fridge.

3. What is kept under the sink?

    A) soap   B) food

    C) spoons   D) lunch

4. What does Lydia want to do after the dishes have been put away?

    A) She goes to the office.   B) She takes it easy.

    C) She eats lunch.   D) She washes the dishes.

5. Where was Uncle George's dog during lunch?

A) in the bathroom　　　　B) in the backyard

C) in the kitchen　　　　D) in the cupboard

 測驗題庫中譯

1. 麗迪亞和她的喬治姨丈午餐後做什麼？

A) 他們清理廚房。　　　　B) 他們去上班。

C) 他們去散步。　　　　D) 他們吃了些三明治。

2. 麗迪亞最先做什麼事情？

A) 她洗碗盤。　　B) 她把碗盤擦乾。

C) 她清理桌子。　　　　D) 她把剩菜剩飯放進冰箱。

3. 放在水槽下的是什麼東西？

A) 肥皂　　　　B) 食物

C) 湯匙　　　　D) 午餐

4. 當碗盤都清理乾淨後，麗迪亞想做什麼？

A) 去上班　　　B) 放輕鬆

C) 吃午餐　　　D) 洗碗盤

5. 午餐期間喬治姨丈的狗在哪裡呢？

A) 在浴室裡面　　B) 在後院

C) 在廚房裡面　　D) 在櫥櫃裡面

Unit 4 Lydia's Letter

Dear Mark,

How are you? I'll bet you're surprised that I'm writing you a letter instead of sending an email to you! Well, I have a good excuse. My aunt and uncle have a laptop computer, which my uncle uses to work on. He took it with him to the office, so now I have no way to contact you, other than by regular mail.

Everything here is good so far. My aunt and uncle have told me to make myself at home, and I have. The room I am staying in is their guest room, but already it feels like mine. I have put pictures up on the wall to remind me of home and all of my friends.

I haven't done much yet. I'm just taking it easy. Today I slept in late, and had a nice lunch with my uncle. Then I watched a bit of TV—but not too much. Watching TV is hard work when the shows are in English, and there are no subtitles!

Today I also made a new friend—a dog named Pepper! He belongs to my aunt and uncle, and this afternoon I took him out for a walk. He's a big dog, and quite strong. In fact, I want to take back what I just said. I didn't take him for a walk–he took me!

Oh! I hear the front door opening! That means that either my aunt or uncle is home from work. I don't want to be rude, so I will go and say hello.

Write back soon!

Lydia

麗迪亞的信

親愛的馬克：

你好嗎？我打賭你一定很訝異我不是寫電子信件給你，反而是寄手寫的信。這個嘛，我有很好的理由。我阿姨和姨丈有一個筆記型電腦，是我姨丈工作時要用的。他把它帶去上班，所以我現在沒辦法聯絡你，只好靠手寫的信囉。

到目前為止這裡一切都很好。我阿姨和姨丈要我把這裡當成自己的家，而我也那麼做了。我住的房間是他們的客房，但我感覺就像是我自己的房間一樣。我已經在牆上掛上照片，讓我想起我的家和朋友。

我還沒有太多活動，只是讓自己放輕鬆罷了。今天我睡過頭了，而且跟我姨丈吃了一頓很棒的午餐。然後我看了一下電視，不過沒有看太久。當所有節目都是說英文時，看電視實在太難了，況且也

沒有字幕說明。

　今天我還認識了一個新朋友——一隻叫做胡椒的狗。牠是我阿姨和姨丈養的，今天下午我帶牠出去散步。牠是隻很大的狗，而且相當強壯。事實上，我要收回我剛剛說的話——並不是我帶牠出去散步，而是牠帶我出去。

　喔，我聽到前門打開的聲音了，那表示姨丈或阿姨下班回來了。我不想表現得沒有禮貌，所以我得下去打聲招呼了。趕快回信喲！

麗迪亞

Vocabulary

excuse	藉口；理由
laptop computer	筆記型電腦
contact	接觸；聯絡
regular	常態的；一般的；有規則的
remind	提醒；使想起
subtitle	副標；字幕
quite	相當；非常
rude	無禮的；粗魯的

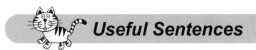 **Useful Sentences**

◎ I'll bet **我敢說**

used to say that one thinks something is true
用以說明一個人確信某事是真的

A: I'm going to give my girlfriend a dozen roses for her birthday.
我女朋友生日時我要送她十二朵玫瑰花。

B: That's so nice of you! I'll bet she really loves them.
你真好！我敢說她一定會愛死那些玫瑰花的。

◎ So far **目前**

up to this point in time
直到目前為止

A: Have you been able to fix the computer yet?
你可以修理好電腦嗎？

B: No. So far I've had no luck with it.
不行。到目前為止我都還搞不定它。

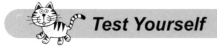 **Test Yourself**

1. Why is Lydia writing a letter to Mark?

   A) She loves him.

   B) She can't send him an email.

   C) The phone is broken.

   D) The computer is broken.

2. What can we say about Uncle George's computer?

   A) It is too heavy to carry.

   B) It is not working right now.

   C) It is what he uses to work on.

   D) It always stays in his house.

3. What does Lydia do after lunch?

   A) She watches TV.   B) She goes for a walk.

   C) She writes an email.   D) She goes to sleep.

4. Why is watching TV difficult for Lydia?

   A) Because there are no subtitles.

   B) Because she can't turn the TV on.

   C) Because her eyes are bad.

   D) Because she has seen all the programs before.

5. What is the name of Lydia's new friend?

   A) Mark　　　　　　　　　B) George

   C) Pepper　　　　　　　　　D) Salt

 測驗題庫中譯

1. 為什麼麗迪亞以手寫信給馬克呢？

   A) 因為她愛他　　　　　　B) 她無法寄電子郵件給他

   C) 電話壞掉了　　　　　　D) 電腦壞掉了

2. 我們可以怎麼形容喬治姨丈的電腦呢？

   A) 它太重了提不動　　　　B) 它現在故障了

   C) 它是他工作的工具　　　D) 它一直放在家中

3. 麗迪亞午餐後做什麼事情呢？

   A) 她看電視　　　　　　　B) 她去散步

   C) 她寫一封電子郵件　　　D) 她去睡覺

4. 為什麼看電視對麗迪亞來說很困難？

   A) 因為沒有字幕　　　　　B) 因為她無法打開電視機

   C) 因為她眼睛不好　　　　D) 因為她之前已經看過所有的節目了

5. 麗迪亞的新朋友叫什麼名字？

   A) 馬克　　B) 喬治　　C) 胡椒　　D) 鹽巴

Unit 5 Lydia Meets Her Cousin

Lydia walks into the kitchen and sees her cousin, Eric.

Lydia : Eric?

Eric : Lydia! Long time, no see!

Lydia : I'll say! It's been three years. I hardly recognize you. You're so tall!

Eric : And you! You look great without your braces!

Lydia : There's something else that's different about you. It isn't your hair... I know! You aren't wearing glasses!

Eric : You've got a good memory!

Lydia : I would love to give up my glasses. Only I don't like contact lenses. I'm afraid of sticking anything in my eye.

Eric : Really? Then you should do what I did.

Lydia : What's that?

Eric : Laser eye surgery. A doctor uses a laser and fixes your eyes. You can kiss your glasses goodbye!

Lydia : Really? Wow! That must be expensive.

Eric : It's not cheap, that's for sure, but it' was worth it.

Lydia : Why is that?

Eric : Well, when I played baseball before, my glasses always got in the way. Now that I don't have them, I'm a better player than ever!

Lydia and Eric continue their conversation.

Lydia : Speaking of baseball, when am I going to get a chance to see you play?

Eric : Well, I have a game tonight. Are you interested in cheering me on?

Lydia : Am I?! I've been looking forward to seeing you play for ages.

Eric :   Really?

Lydia :   Yep. You are the family pride! Everyone talks about what a great pitcher you are.

Eric :   The family in Taiwan talks about it?

Lydia :   And so do our relatives in Hong Kong and China! You're something of a celebrity. Everyone thinks it would be so cool if you wound up in the majors!

Eric :   It's my dream, too. But I have a long way to go.

Lydia :   Don't worry! We'll all be proud of you no matter what happens!

麗迪亞見到表哥

麗迪亞走進廚房，看到她的表哥艾瑞克。

麗迪亞：　艾瑞克？

艾瑞克：　麗迪亞！好久不見！

麗迪亞：　沒錯！已經三年了。我幾乎認不出你來了。你長得

好高！

艾瑞克： 妳也是！沒有牙齒矯正器的妳看起來好極了。

麗迪亞： 你還有一個地方不一樣。不是你的頭髮……我知道了，你沒有戴眼鏡！

艾瑞克： 妳記性可真好！

麗迪亞： 我也不想戴眼鏡。不過我不喜歡隱形眼鏡，我不喜歡東西黏在眼睛裡面的感覺。

艾瑞克： 是嗎？那你應該學學我。

麗迪亞： 是什麼？

艾瑞克： 雷射矯正手術。醫生利用雷射矯正你的視力，以後你就不用再戴眼鏡了。

麗迪亞： 真的嗎？哇，那一定很貴吧。

艾瑞克： 貴，那是當然了，不過很值得。

麗迪亞： 為什麼呢？

艾瑞克： 這個嘛，以前我打棒球時，眼鏡總是礙手礙腳的。現在我沒戴眼鏡，當然就比以前打得更好了。

麗迪亞和艾瑞克繼續談話。

麗迪亞： 說到棒球，我什麼時候有機會去看你打球呢？

艾瑞克： 這個啊，今天晚上我有場比賽。妳有興趣來加油嗎？

麗迪亞： 有興趣！？我早就一直期待著要看你比賽了！

艾瑞克： 真的嗎？

麗迪亞：　是啊。你是家族的驕傲！每個人都在說你是一個多
　　　　　棒的投手。

艾瑞克：　臺灣的親友這麼說?

麗迪亞：　還有我們在香港以及大陸的親戚。你是個大名人
　　　　　呢。每個人都覺得如果你能打進大聯盟，那就太酷
　　　　　了。

艾瑞克：　那也是我的夢想，不過我還要再加油呢。

麗迪亞：　別擔心。不管怎樣，我們都是以你為榮的。

 **Vocabulary**

recognize	辨認；認出
braces	齒列矯正器
memory	記憶力
contact lens	隱形眼鏡
laser	雷射
surgery	外科手術
cheer somebody on	為某人加油

look forward to something	期待某事
pride	驕傲
pitcher	棒球投手
relatives	親戚
celebrity	名聲；名望
wind up	向上攀爬

 **Useful Sentences**

◎ Kiss something goodbye 告別

to know that somebody or something will be gone from one's life forever
某人或某事即將從一個人的生活中永遠消失

A: Why should I buy this soap? What's so special about it?
我為什麼要買這個肥皂？它有什麼特別的嗎？

B: With this soap, you can kiss stains on your clothes goodbye!
有了這種肥皂，妳就可以對衣服上的污漬永遠說再見了。

◎ Be worth it **值得**

to know that doing something, although it may not be easy or cheap, is a good thing to do
意謂著某事即使過程困難或者所費不貲還是相當值得的

A: I don't know why you spend so much time studying.
我不懂你為什麼要花這麼多時間唸書。

B: One day, when I get into a famous university, I know it will be worth it.
等到我考上了一所知名大學，這一切都會是值得的。

◎ Get in the way **妨礙；阻止**

to be something or someone that prevents one from doing something or prevents something from happening
阻礙某人，或防止某事發生

A: So why don't you and Joe just go on a date?
為什麼你和喬不繼續交往呢？

B: I want to, but there's never time. School work keeps getting in the way!
我想啊，但是沒有時間。課業老是卡在中間。

◎ Look forward to something　**期待**

to think that it will be good when something happens in the future
對某事的發生或到來充滿樂觀的期待

A: Are you looking forward to going to university?
你想上大學嗎？

B: I am. I'm very excited about it.
想啊。我已經迫不及待。

◎ Have a long way to go　**還有很長一段路**

to need to do a lot of work before something happens 意指在達成某事之前還需要許多努力

A: I wish that there were a cure for the common cold!
我真希望流行感冒有藥可治。

B: So do I! Unfortunately, science has a long way to go.
我也是！不幸地，科學界也還在努力當中。

◎ No matter what **無論如何**

used to say that something will definitely happen
指不論發生什麼事，都不會影響

A: Will you still want to kiss me when I have braces?
我戴牙套時，你還會想吻我嗎？

B: I'd want to kiss you no matter what! Braces aren't important.
不論如何我都想吻妳，牙套根本不是重點。

Test Yourself

1. Where does Lydia first meet her cousin?

   A) in the bathroom   B) at the front door

   C) in the hallway   D) in the kitchen

2. Which of the following is true of Lydia and Eric?

   A) They have never met before.

   B) It has been a long time since they first met.

   C) They are not happy to see one another.

   D) They are not really cousins.

3. In which of the following places do members of Lydia and Eric's family live?

    A) L.A.   B) Hong Kong

    C) China   D) All of the above

4. When does Eric have a baseball game?

    A) tonight   B) tomorrow

    C) yesterday   D) next week

5. What does Eric invite Lydia to do?

    A) go out for dinner   B) wash the dishes

    C) meet his friends   D) watch him play baseball

 測驗題庫中譯

1. 麗迪亞一開始在哪裡碰到他表哥？

    A) 在浴室裡   B) 在前門

    C) 在走廊上   D) 在廚房裡

2. 下列關於麗迪亞和他表哥的敘述何者正確？

    A) 他們以前從沒見過彼此   B) 他們已經很久沒見面了

    C) 他們不高興見到彼此   D) 他們不是親表兄妹

3. 麗迪亞和艾瑞克的家族成員，有居住在下列哪個地方？

A) 洛杉磯　　　　　　　　　B) 香港

C) 中國大陸　　　　　　　　D) 以上皆是

4. 艾瑞克何時有棒球比賽？

A) 今天晚上　　　　　　　　B) 明天

C) 昨天　　　　　　　　　　D) 下星期

5. 艾瑞克邀請麗迪亞做什麼呢？

A) 出去吃晚餐　　　　　　　B) 洗碗盤

C) 和他的朋友見面　　　　　D) 看他打棒球

Unit 6
Let's Play Ball!

Lydia and her aunt and uncle are at Eric's baseball game. They are thirsty, so Lydia's aunt goes to get some drinks.

Lydia : Eric is playing really well tonight, isn't he?

Uncle George : I'll say. All that practice is really paying off.

Lydia : Oh, look! He's up to bat.

Uncle George : Come on, Eric! You can do it!

Lydia : It's too bad aunt June isn't here to see this!

Uncle George : Maybe not. Eric just got a strike.

Lydia : Come on, Eric!

Uncle George : The pitcher is winding up...

Lydia : Eric swings and—

Uncle George : Oh my! That just may be a home run!

Lydia : It is! It is a home run!

Uncle George : Way to go! Eric! High five!

Aunt June comes back with sodas for everyone.

Aunt June :　Did I miss anything?

Uncle George : Did you? Only our son hitting a home run!

Aunt June :　He didn't!

Uncle George : He did! You should have seen it. The ball went right out of the park.

Aunt June :　That's my boy! So what's the score now?

Uncle George : Well, there was a runner on second base when Eric was up to bat, so his hit scored two runs.

Aunt June :　So our team is winning?

Uncle George : That's right!

Aunt June :　What an exciting match!

咱們打球去！

　麗迪亞和阿姨及姨丈在艾瑞克的棒球賽上。他們很渴，因此麗迪亞的阿姨去買一些飲料。

麗迪亞：　　艾瑞克今晚真的打得很好，對吧？

喬治姨丈：我同意。所有的練習都值得了。

麗迪亞： 喔，看哪！他要揮棒了。

喬治姨丈：加油，艾瑞克，你一定辦得到。

麗迪亞： 真可惜，茱兒阿姨沒看到這一幕。

喬治姨丈：還不一定。艾瑞克揮棒落空了。

麗迪亞： 加油，艾瑞克。

喬治姨丈：投手正彎身準備……

麗迪亞： 艾瑞克揮棒……

喬治姨丈：喔，天啊！可能是全壘打。

麗迪亞： 沒錯！是全壘打！

喬治姨丈：艾瑞克，太棒了！萬歲！

茱兒阿姨帶著大家的汽水回來了。

茱兒阿姨：我錯過什麼了嗎？

喬治姨丈：有嗎？只不過是妳兒子打出一支全壘打罷了！

茱兒阿姨：不可能！

喬治姨丈：是真的。妳應該看看的，球直飛場外呢。

茱兒阿姨：真不愧是我兒子！那現在比數怎樣了？

喬治姨丈：這個嘛，當艾瑞克揮棒時剛好二壘有人，所以他擊
出了兩分全壘打。

茱兒阿姨：所以我們這隊贏了？

喬治姨丈：沒錯！

茱兒阿姨：真讓人熱血沸騰！

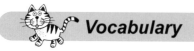 **Vocabulary**

thirsty	口渴的
be up to bat	準備揮棒
strike	打擊；揮棒落空
wind up	彎身；彎曲
swing	揮動
home run	全壘打
high five	拍手歡呼
soda	蘇打；汽水
score	分數；得分
base	壘包
run	跑步
match	競賽；比賽

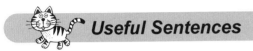 **Useful Sentences**

◎ Pay off 有所回報

beginning to show positive results
開始呈現正面的結果

A: So you are finally dating Betty?
那你終於跟貝蒂約會囉？

B: Yep. At first I thought she didn't like me, but I kept trying. It seems that my patience has finally paid off!
是啊。一開始我覺得她不喜歡我，但我還是繼續努力。似乎是我的耐心終於得到回報了。

◎ Way to go! 做得好

a phrase used to express approval to somebody for something they have just done
這個片語用以表示贊同某人剛做的某事

A: Guess what? I won my school's speech contest and next week I'll compete against students from other schools.
你知道嗎？我贏了學校的演講比賽，所以下禮拜要參加校際比賽了。

B: Way to go! I knew you could do it!
太好了！我就知道你辦得到。

 **Test Yourself**

1. When Eric hits his home run, what is his mother doing?
   A) making dinner   B) watching the game on TV
   C) ignoring him   D) getting drinks for everyone

2. What did Aunt June buy?
   A) beer   B) sodas
   C) milk   D) juice

3. What did Aunt June miss?
   A) Eric's home run   B) thc whole game
   C) Eric's big mistake   D) the drinks

4. Who's team is winning?
   A) Eric's   B) Uncle George's
   C) Aunt June's   D) Lydia's

5. What does Aunt June think about the match?

    A) it is over   B) it is boring

    C) it is useless   D) it is interesting

 測驗題庫中譯

1. 當艾瑞克打出全壘打時，她的媽媽在做什麼？

    A) 做晚餐   B) 看電視轉播比賽

    C) 不理會他   D) 替大家買飲料

2. 茱兒阿姨買了什麼東西？

    A) 啤酒   B) 汽水

    C) 牛奶   D) 果汁

3. 茱兒阿姨錯過了什麼？

    A) 艾瑞克的全壘打   B) 整場比賽

    C) 艾瑞克的大錯誤   D) 飲料

4. 誰的隊伍贏了？

    A) 艾瑞克的   B) 喬治姨丈的

    C) 茱兒阿姨的   D) 麗迪亞的

5. 茱兒阿姨認為比賽怎麼樣？

    A) 結束了   B) 很無聊

    C) 沒有用處   D) 很有趣

Unit 7 After the Game

Eric runs up to his mother, father, and Lydia after the game.

Eric:	Hey guys!
Aunt June :	Eric! What a great game! We're so proud of you, honey.
Eric :	Did you see my home run? What did you think of that?
Aunt June :	Umm, er...
Eric :	Can we get anything to eat? I'm so hungry I could eat a horse!
Aunt June :	Well, I suppose we could go out for a bite to eat. We can make it a celebration!
Eric :	Cool!
Aunt June :	We can go anywhere you want. Where would you like to go?
Eric :	How about McDonalds?
Aunt June :	McDonalds?
Eric :	Mmm, I could eat five hamburgers!
Aunt June :	Well, OK, if you like...
Eric :	We can go through the drive-thru. That way, when we get home we can watch

the NBA game that's playing tonight.

Aunt June :   Ah, my son! Always thinking about
sports! And his stomach!

The family gets into the car. Uncle George is driving, and Aunt June is in the front seat.

Uncle George :   Hmm. I'm not so familiar with this
part of town. Where is the nearest
McDonalds?

Aunt June :   I think there's one on Main Street, just
past the next set of lights.

Uncle George :   I don't see it ...

Aunt June :   Maybe after the next set of lights.
Keep driving.

Uncle George :   Maybe we should just go to another
restaurant.

Aunt June :   Keep driving! See?

Uncle George :   No - ah, there it is!

Aunt June :   There it was! You just drove right
past it!

比賽之後

比賽之後艾瑞克跑去找他的媽媽、爸爸和麗迪亞。

艾瑞克：　嘿，大夥兒！

茱兒阿姨：艾瑞克！很棒的比賽！親愛的，我們都以你為榮。

艾瑞克：　你看到我的全壘打了嗎？你覺得怎麼樣？

茱兒阿姨：這個，嗯……

艾瑞克：　我們可以去吃點東西嗎？我餓死了。

茱兒阿姨：嗯，我想我們可以出去吃點東西，就當做是慶祝。

艾瑞克：　太棒了！

茱兒阿姨：只要你高興，去哪吃都行。你想去哪呢？

艾瑞克：　麥當勞怎麼樣？

茱兒阿姨：麥當勞？

艾瑞克：　嗯，我可以吃掉五個漢堡。

茱兒阿姨：喔，好啊，如果你想的話……

艾瑞克：　我們可以從「得來速」買，這樣的話，我們回到家
　　　　　還來得及看今天晚上的 NBA 籃球賽。

茱兒阿姨：喔，這個兒子啊！只知道運動跟吃的。

這家人坐進車裡。喬治姨丈開車，茱兒阿姨坐在前座。

喬治姨丈：嗯，我對這區不熟，最近的麥當勞在哪裡？

茱兒阿姨：我想中央大街上有一家，就在下一個紅綠燈過去。

喬治姨丈：我沒看到……

茱兒阿姨：也許是在下一個紅綠燈。繼續開。

喬治姨丈：也許我們應該找另一家餐廳。

茱兒阿姨：繼續開車。看到了嗎？

喬治姨丈：沒有……哈，在「這」裡。

茱兒阿姨：是在「那」裡。你開過頭了。

Vocabulary

run up to somebody or something	跑向某人或某物
proud	驕傲的
celebration	慶祝
drive--- thru	得來速
stomach	胃
set of something	一組事物
light	燈
past	通過；超過

Useful Sentences

◎ **How about** 如何

used when one wants to make a suggestion to do something
提議時的用語

A: I'm bored. I don't want to study any more!
我好無聊哦！我不想再唸書了。

B: Me neither. How about we take a break and watch some TV?
我也是。休息一下，看個電視怎麼樣？

◎ **That way** 這樣一來；那樣的話

used to explain how something just mentioned will work well
用以解釋之前提到的事情將會產生的功效

A: If you need anything, I can pick it up for you at the store.
如果你需要任何東西，我可以到店裡幫你買。

B: Thanks! That way, I'll save lots of time!
謝謝，這樣一來，我就節省了很多時間。

◎ A bite to eat 吃一些

something to eat, usually a snack or a small meal
通常是指點心或小份餐點

A: What are you doing after work today?
今天下班後你要做什麼？

B: Not much. I'll probably just grab a bite to eat and then go home.
沒什麼。可能會去吃點東西，然後就回家吧。

◎ Be so hungry one could eat a horse 餓到可以吃下一匹馬

to be very hungry
指非常餓

A: You've been so busy today! Did you have time to eat lunch?
你今天一直很忙。你有時間吃午餐嗎？

B: No. I'm so hungry I could eat a horse.
沒有。我餓得可以吃下一匹馬了。

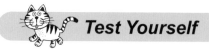

Test Yourself

1. How does Eric feel after the game?

    A) hungry   B) tired

    C) angry   D) surprised

2. How does Aunt June feel when Eric says he wants to go to McDonalds?

    A) hungry   B) tired

    C) angry   D) surprised

3. Who drives the car?

    A) Uncle George   B) Aunt June

    C) Lydia   D) Eric

4. Where does Aunt June say McDonalds is?

    A) at the park   B) near their home

    C) by the restaurant   D) on Main street

5. What mistake does Uncle George make?

    A) He finds the restaurant.

    B) He goes past the restaurant.

    C) He sees the restaurant.

    D) He eats at the restaurant.

 測驗題庫中譯

1. 比賽之後艾瑞克覺得怎樣？

    A) 很餓   B) 很累   C) 生氣   D) 驚訝

2. 當艾瑞克說要去吃麥當勞時，茱兒阿姨覺得怎樣？

    A) 很餓   B) 很累   C) 生氣   D) 驚訝

3. 誰開車？

    A) 喬治姨丈   B) 茱兒阿姨   C) 麗迪亞   D) 艾瑞克

4. 茱兒阿姨說麥當勞在哪裡？

    A) 在公園裡面   B) 他們家附近 C) 餐廳隔壁   D) 在中央大街上

5. 喬治姨丈犯了什麼錯誤？

    A) 他找到餐館   B) 他開車超過了餐館

    C) 他看到餐館   D) 他在餐館裡曲吃東西

Unit 8 At McDonalds

The family's car is in the line outside the drive-thru.

Uncle George : OK, now before we go through the drive-thru, I want everyone to write down what they want on this piece of paper, OK?

Aunt June : Here's a pen, kids! Write quickly. We're next in line!

Uncle George pulls up next to the speaker so that he can give the family's order.

Clerk : Welcome to McDonalds. Can I...

Uncle George : Pardon me? I can't hear you!

Clerk : Sorry sir! Can I take your order?

Uncle George : Yes. Let's see. We'll have three cheeseburgers, and two hamburgers.

Clerk : Any fries with that?

Uncle George : Yes, four large orders of fries.

Clerk : Anything to drink?

Uncle George : Yes, three cokes, and one vanilla milkshake.

Clerk :	Will that be all?
Uncle George :	Yes.
Clerk :	The total comes to sixteen dollars and forty-five cents. If you'll please drive up to the next window, your order will be ready in just a minute.
Uncle George :	Thank you!

Uncle George drives up to the next window.

Clerk :	Here's your order, sir. The total is sixteen forty-five.
Uncle George :	Here's a twenty.
Clerk :	Thank you. Three dollars and fifty- five cents is your change.
Uncle George :	Excuse me, may I have some extra ketchup and some more napkins?
Clerk :	Sure! Here you go! Have a nice day!

在麥當勞

這家人的車子在得來速外面排隊。

喬治姨丈：　好吧，現在，在我們通過得來速以前，請每個人都把你想要吃的東西寫在這張紙上，好嗎？

茱兒阿姨：　孩子們，這裡有筆。快點寫下來，要輪到我們了！

喬治姨丈把車停在麥克風旁邊，這樣他才可以幫家人點餐。

店　員：　歡迎來到麥當勞。我可以……

喬治姨丈：　請再說一次好嗎？我聽不清楚。

店　員：　抱歉，先生。我可以幫你點餐嗎？

喬治姨丈：　好，讓我看看。我們要三個起司堡，還有兩個漢堡。

店　員：　要附薯條嗎？

喬治姨丈：　要，四個大薯條。

店　員：　要什麼飲料嗎？

喬治姨丈：　三杯可樂，還有一個香草奶昔。

店　員：　這樣就好了嗎？

喬治姨丈：　是的。

店　員：　總共是十六塊四十五分錢。請你開車到下一個窗口，餐點馬上就會好了。

喬治姨丈：　謝謝！

喬治姨丈把車開到下一個窗口。

店員： 這是你的餐點，先生。總共是十六塊四十五分。

喬治姨丈： 這是二十塊錢。

店員： 謝謝。找你三塊錢五十五分。

喬治姨丈： 不好意思，我可以多拿一些番茄醬和紙巾嗎？

店員： 當然，這些給你，祝你有個愉快的一天！

Vocabulary

line	線條；隊伍
write down	寫下來
pull up	停下來
speaker	麥克風；擴音器
welcome	歡迎
order	點餐
cheeseburger	起司漢堡
fries	薯條
coke	可樂

vanilla	香草
milkshake	奶昔
change	改變
extra	額外的
ketchup	番茄醬
napkin	紙巾

 **Useful Sentences**

◎ A piece of something 一片

usually a small item or a portion of a larger item (example: a piece of pizza)
通常指一個小東西或者一個較大物體當中的一小部份
（例如：一片披薩）

A: That man just threw a piece of garbage on the ground!
那個男的居然隨手亂丟垃圾！

B: How rude! I'm going to go tell him to pick it up!
真沒水準！我要去叫他撿起來！

◎ Pardon me 再說一次

the same as "excuse me", which explains a request for others to repeat
同「excuse me」，用來請求他人重複所言

A: Hello, may I please speak to John? ... Hello?
哈囉，可以請約翰聽電話嗎？……哈囉？

B: Pardon me? I can hardly hear you. This phone line is very bad!
可以再說一次嗎？我聽不清楚。這支電話線很糟。

A: May I please speak to John?
可以請約翰聽電話嗎？

B: Oh, okay. I can hear you better now.
喔，好的。我現在聽得比較清楚了。

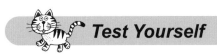 **Test Yourself**

1. How many cheeseburgers does Uncle George order?

   A) one   B) two

   C) three   D) four

2. Which of the following does Uncle George not order?

   A) a hamburger   B) fries

   C) a chicken sandwich   D) coke

3. What kind of milkshake does Uncle George want?

   A) a vanilla one   B) a hot one

   C) a cheese one   D) a large one

4. How much money does Uncle George give to the clerk?

A) ten dollars

B) twenty dollars

C) thirty dollars

D) forty dollars

5. Before he drives away, what does Uncle George ask the clerk for?

A) ketchup and napkins

B) cheeseburgers

C) directions

D) his change

 測驗題庫中譯

1. 喬治姨丈點了多少個漢堡？

   A) 一個　　　B) 兩個　　　C) 三個　　　D) 四個

2. 下列何者是喬治姨丈沒有點的東西？

   A) 一個漢堡　　B) 薯條　　C) 一個雞肉三明治 D) 可樂

3. 喬治姨丈想要哪種奶昔？

   A) 香草奶昔　　B) 熱奶昔　　C) 起司奶昔　　D) 大杯奶昔

4. 喬治姨丈給了多少錢給店員？

   A) 十兩塊錢　　B) 二十塊錢　　C) 三十塊錢　　D) 四十塊錢

5. 在他開走之前，喬治姨丈向店員要了什麼東西？

   A) 番茄醬和紙巾　B) 起士漢堡　C) 問路　　　D) 找錢

Chapter ② All About Eric
關於愛瑞克

Unit 1 Eric's Dream

Eric is Lydia's sixteen-year-old cousin. As you know, he's a great baseball player, and he has quite an appetite. This summer, though, is not all fun and games for Eric. While he'd like nothing better than to play baseball all day, Eric has to go to summer school.

It's eight o'clock, and Eric's alarm clock is ringing. He doesn't want to get out of bed. He'd like to sleep in, just like his friends can. However, Eric must wake up. He has to shower and eat his breakfast, and if he doesn't hurry, he'll be late for summer school.

Eric goes to the bathroom and has his shower. He hopes it will wake him up. He is feeling very tired this morning, for two reasons: the main reason is because he stayed up too late last night. He and Lydia had rented some DVD's from the local video store. They watched a comedy, an action movie, and a horror movie. By the time they'd watched all three, it was almost two am!

The second reason why Eric is so tired this morning is because of his dreams. They were all very bad. In one of them, Eric was playing baseball. He was up to bat, and every time the pitcher threw the ball, there was some problem, and he couldn't hit it. One time, the ball the pitcher threw was the size of a grain of rice. Eric couldn't see it, and so he got a strike. The next ball the pitcher threw was as big as a watermelon. Eric felt scared when the pitcher threw it and had to jump out of the way.

It's no wonder that Eric feels tired this morning. But while he'd like nothing better than to stay in bed all morning, he can't. It's already eight-thirty, and class starts in an hour.

艾瑞克的夢

　　艾瑞克是麗迪亞的表哥，今年十六歲。就如同你所知道的，他是個很棒的棒球選手，而且食量相當大。但是，今年夏天對艾瑞克而言並非充滿了趣味和歡樂。當艾瑞克一整天除了打棒球，其他什麼事情都不想做時，他卻得去參加暑期課程。

　　已經八點了，艾瑞克的鬧鐘正在響著，他不想起床。他想要睡覺，就像他的其他朋友一樣。然而，艾瑞克必須起床。他得去沖澡然後吃早餐，而且如果他不快一點的話，他的暑期輔導課就會遲到。

　　艾瑞克走進浴室淋浴，他希望那樣能使他清醒過來。今天早上他感覺相當疲累，理由有二：主要的原因是因為昨晚他熬夜得太晚了。他和麗迪亞在附近的影帶出租店租了一些DVD，他們看了一齣喜劇、一齣動作片還有一部恐怖片。當他們看完了三部片之後，已經幾乎凌晨兩點鐘了。

　　第二個讓艾瑞克這麼疲累的原因，是他作的夢。那些夢境都不太好。其中一個夢是，艾瑞克正在打棒球，他握著球棒。每當投手把球投出來時，總是會出現問題使他無法打到球。有一次，投手投出來的球像一粒米一樣大，艾瑞克看不到它，所以他揮棒落空了。投手投出來的下一個球，則像西瓜一樣大，當投手把球丟出來時，艾瑞克覺得很害怕而必須跳開。

　　難怪艾瑞克今天早上覺得很累。但是當他想要一整個早上都躺在床上什麼都不做時，他卻不能。已經八點半了，而一個小時後就要開始上課了。

 *Vocabulary*

alarm clock	鬧鐘
ring	鈴響
sleep in	睡懶覺
wake up	醒來；清醒過來
shower	淋浴
reason	理由；原因
rent	承租
DVD	多功能影音光碟
local	當地的
grain	穀類
strike	打擊；揮棒落空

Useful Sentences

◎ As...as... 如同

used for comparison, to show that one thing is like another in some way
用來比較某事的類似點

A: Your hands are as cold as ice!
你的手像冰一樣冷！

B: I know! I forgot to take my gloves with me today.
我知道！我今天忘了戴我的手套了。

◎ It's no wonder that... 難怪

to not be surprising
沒有什麼好訝異的

A: I left my umbrella on the bus. Then, as I was walking home, it began to rain!
我把傘忘在公車上，後來我走路回家時，就開始下雨了。

B: It's no wonder that you're all wet! I'll get you a towel.
難怪妳全身都濕了。我去拿條毛巾給妳。

 **Review Questions**

1. What time does Eric wake up?

    A) two o'clock   B) eight o'clock

    C) eight-thirty   D) nine-thirty

2. What does Eric have to do before he goes to school?

    A) finish his homework   B) take a shower

    C) go to sleep   D) eat lunch

3. Which of the following movies did Lydia and Eric not watch?

    A) a comedy   B) an action movie

    C) a horror movie   D) a romance

4. For what reason, besides staying up late, is Eric tired?

    A) He ate too much.

    B) He forgot to turn his alarm clock off.

    C) He has summer school in the morning.

    D) He had bad dreams.

5. What was Eric doing in his dream?
   A) playing baseball   B) sleeping
   C) doing his homework   D) taking a shower

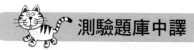 測驗題庫中譯

1. 艾瑞克什麼時候醒來？
   A) 兩點鐘   B) 八點鐘   C) 八點半   D) 九點半

2. 在艾瑞克到學校之前，他必須做什麼事情？
   A 做完回家功課   B)) 淋浴   C) 去睡覺   D) 吃午餐

3. 下列哪種電影是麗迪亞和艾瑞克沒有看的？
   A) 一齣喜劇   B) 一部動作片
   C) 一部恐怖片   D) 浪漫愛情片

4. 除了熬夜到很晚之外，是什麼原因使得艾瑞克覺得很累？
   A) 他吃的太多了   B) 他忘記把鬧鐘關掉
   C) 他早上有暑期課程   D) 他做了惡夢

5. 在艾瑞克的夢裡面，他在做什麼事情？
   A) 打棒球   B) 睡覺
   C) 做家庭作業回家功課   D) 淋浴

Unit 2 Summer School

Eric is finishing up his breakfast when Aunt June walks in.

Aunt June : Hurry up, slow poke! You'll be late.

Eric : I'm almost done eating my breakfast.

Aunt June : Speaking of breakfast — what is that you're eating?

Eric : Leftover pizza.

Aunt June : Pizza? Why don't you eat some cereal or fruit?

Eric : Well, I already had a bowl of cereal. But I was still hungry, and I saw the pizza in the fridge.

Aunt June : You're a strange boy, but I love you. I'll put your lunch in your school bag. Did you remember your homework?

Eric : Uh... huh.

Aunt June : OK. I'll warm up the car. I'll be waiting in the driveway for you.

Eric : Thanks, Mom. I'll be right out.

Aunt June has just dropped Eric off at school. He meets his friend, Kimberly as he is walking into the building.

Kimberly :   Hey, Eric! How's it going?

Eric :   Not bad. Though on a day like today, I'd much rather be playing baseball, or sleeping...

Kimberly :   ... or swimming, or hanging out with friends. Anything but school, right?

Eric :   Tell me about it. So, did you finish your assignment?

Kimberly :   Yes, I don't usually like writing essays, but this topic was interesting.

Eric :   I thought so too! Being in summer school isn't fun, but at least our assignments aren't boring!

The bell has rung, and the students are listening to their teacher, Miss Jones.

Miss Jones : Eric? Eric? ERIC!

Eric :   Yes, Miss Jones?

Miss Jones : Did you hear what I just said?

Eric : Um... pardon me, Miss Jones. I missed that.

Miss Jones : I've asked everyone to pass their assignments to the front of the class.

Eric : Oh! It's in my bag... just a moment! Here it is.

Miss Jones : Thank you Eric. When class lets out for lunch, I'd like you to stay behind for a minute. There's something I'd like to discuss with you.

Eric : OK, Miss Jones.

Miss Jones : But first things first, Eric; your assignment. Please bring it to me.

Eric : Yes, Miss Jones. Here it is.

暑期課程

當茉兒阿姨走進來時，艾瑞克正好吃完早餐。

茉兒阿姨：快點，慢郎中！你要遲到了。

艾瑞克： 我快要吃完早餐了。

茉兒阿姨：説到早餐，你在吃什麼？

艾瑞克：　　剩下的披薩啊。

茱兒阿姨：披薩？為什麼不吃一些麥片或水果呢？

艾瑞克：　　喔，我已經吃了一碗麥片了，但我還是很餓，所以我才吃冰箱裡面的披薩。

茱兒阿姨：你真是個奇怪的男孩，不過我還是很愛你。我會把你的　午餐放進書包裡面。你有記得做回家功課嗎？

艾瑞克：　　嗯。

茱兒阿姨：好，我去準備發動車子。我會在車道上等你。

艾瑞克：　　謝謝妳，媽，我馬上就好。

　　茱兒阿姨剛把艾瑞克送到學校。在他走進大樓時，他遇見他的朋友金柏莉。

金柏莉：　　嘿，艾瑞克！最近過得怎樣？

艾瑞克：　　還不錯。不過像今天這種日子裡，我寧願打棒球或者睡覺……

金柏莉：　　……或者游泳、跟朋友出去鬼混。什麼都好，就是不要上課，是吧？

艾瑞克：　　一點也沒錯。對了，你做完作業了嗎？

金柏莉：　　做完啦，我不太喜歡寫文章，不過這一次的主題很有趣。

艾瑞克：　　我也這麼覺得。上暑期課程不怎麼好玩，不過至少我們的作業不算無聊。

鐘聲響了，學生們正在聽瓊斯老師說話。

瓊斯小姐： 艾瑞克？艾瑞克？艾一瑞一克！

艾瑞克： 什麼事，瓊斯小姐？

瓊斯小姐： 你聽到我剛剛說的話了嗎？

艾瑞克： 嗯⋯⋯請再說一次，瓊斯小姐，我沒聽到。

瓊斯小姐： 我剛要每個人把作業交到前面來。

艾瑞克： 喔，在我的書包裡面⋯⋯等一下，在這裡。

瓊斯小姐： 謝謝你，艾瑞克，午餐時間時，我希望你留下來一會。有一件事我想和你討論。

艾瑞克： 好的，瓊斯小姐。

瓊斯小姐： 但是眼前的事情先解決，艾瑞克，請把你的作業交給我吧。

艾瑞克： 是，瓊斯小姐。在這兒。

Vocabulary

finish up	結束
slow poke	動作緩慢的人
bowl	碗

cereal	穀類加工食品
warm up	暖身；做準備
driveway	車道
drop off	放下
assignment	作業；指定任務
let out	洩漏；放出去

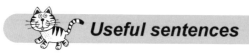 **Useful sentences**

◎ Stay behind 留在原地

to wait for somebody
等待某人

A: Where is Jim? Is he still in the store?
吉姆在哪裡？他還在店裡嗎？

B: I think so. I know you're in a hurry, so you can leave. I'll stay behind until Jim shows up!
我想是吧。我知道你趕時間，你先離開吧。我留下來等吉姆出來。

◎ Tell me about it **還用說**

used to indicate that one completely agrees or understands what somebody has just said
用來表示完全同意或了解某人的話

A: It's so hot today!
今天真熱！

B: Tell me about it. I feel like I'm going to melt!
一點也沒錯。我覺得我快要融化了。

◎ Would rather **寧願**

used to express what somebody would like to do one thing more than something else
用以表示某人較傾向某事的意願

A: Do you want to see an action movie or a comedy tonight?
今天晚上你想要看動作片還是喜劇片？

B: I would rather see a comedy. Action movies are too violent.
我比較想看喜劇片。動作片都太暴力了。

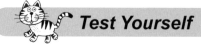 **Test Yourself**

1. What kind of pizza does Eric eat for breakfast?
   A) cheese
   B) leftover
   C) fresh
   D) new

2. How does Eric get to school?
   A) by car
   B) by bus
   C) by train
   D) by bicycle

3. What would Eric rather do than be in school today?
   A) do homework
   B) go swimming
   C) play baseball
   D) write essays

4. What is good about the assignments that Eric and Kimberly get in Miss Jones's class?
   A) They are interesting.
   B) They are finished.
   C) They are boring.
   D) They are difficult.

5. What does Miss Jones want Eric to do?
   A) stop talking so much
   B) listen to her less
   C) keep his homework on his desk
   D) speak to her after class

測驗題庫中譯

1. 艾瑞克吃哪種披薩？

　A) 起司　　　　 B) 剩下的　　 C) 新鮮的　　 D) 新的

2. 艾瑞克怎麼到學校去的？

　A) 搭汽車　　　 B) 搭公車　　 C) 搭火車　　 D) 腳踏車

3. 比起到學校去，艾瑞克今天寧願做什麼？

　A) 寫回家功課　 B) 去游泳　　 C) 打棒球　　 D) 寫論文

4. 艾瑞克和金柏莉認為瓊斯老師出的作業，有什麼優點？

　A) 很有趣　　　 B) 已經做完了 C) 很無聊　　 D) 很困難

5. 瓊斯小姐要艾瑞克做什麼呢？

　A) 不要講那麼多話　　　　 B) 少聽她講課

　C) 把他的作業留在書桌上　 D) 下課後找她談談聊聊

Miss Jones asked her students to write an assignment for homework. The topic was, " If you could be any person in history, who would you be? and why?" Miss Jones told the students to write between 225 and 250 words on this topic. After thinking about it for a long time, Eric decided to write about something he had always dreamed of: flying! Here is what he wrote:

Name: Eric Lin
Date: July 14th

For thousands of years, man looked on birds with envy. Their ability to fly symbolizes freedom. The greatest minds in history worked to give mankind the gift of flight. Even Leonardo da Vinci imagined flying machines. However, it wasn't until the early twentieth century that man realized his greatest dream and it was all due to the work of a pair of brothers, Orville and Wilbur Wright.

Orville and Wilbur Wright grew up in America, the youngest sons in a family of five children. Their parents were very loving and encouraged the boys to do what they do best: dream! Even though they were poor students and dropped out of high school, they were smart and had big ideas.

They wanted to fly. So, instead of getting regular jobs, they began experimenting. They flew kites to see how the wind lifted objects. They built bicycles to understand how machines worked. While many people laughed at these grown men who seemed to play like children, their parents supported them— and we are all very lucky they did.

Through their experiments, the Wright brothers built an airplane and on a cold day in December, 1903, they became the first humans to fly. That's why, if I could be any person in history, I would choose to be one of the Wright brothers. Their courage to dream led to an invention that changed the world, and made mankind's dream to fly like the birds, come true.

艾瑞克的暑期作業

　　瓊斯小姐要學生們寫一篇報告當回家功課。題目是：「如果你可以成為留名歷史的人，你想當誰？為什麼？」瓊斯小姐要學生們根據這個題目寫 225 ～ 250 個字的文章。思考了很久以後，艾瑞克決定寫一件他一直夢想的事情：飛行。以下是他寫的內容：

姓名：艾瑞克・林

日期：七月十四日

　　幾千年以來，人類忌妒地仰望鳥類。牠們的飛行能力象徵著自由。史上最偉大的一些偉人，都致力於賦予人類飛行這個禮物。甚至連李奧納多・達文西都構想過飛行機器。然而，直到二十世紀初期人類才實現這個偉大的夢想，這些都要歸功於一對兄弟的努力：歐維爾・萊特和威爾伯・萊特。

　　歐維爾和威爾伯・萊特在美國長大，同時也是家裡五個孩子中最小的兩個。他們的父母相當慈愛，也很鼓勵他們去追尋他們自己的夢想！即使他們成績不好，還被退學，他們還是相當聰明，而且有很棒的點子。

　　他們想要飛行。因此，他們並沒有去找固定的職業，反而開始做實驗。他們放風箏以觀察風如何將物體提高。他們組拆腳踏車，以便了解機器如何運作。當大家嘲笑著這兩個像在玩孩童遊戲的成年男子，他們的父母卻支持他們——我們很慶幸他們這麼做。

　　在實驗的過程中，萊特兄弟建造了一架飛機，且在 1903 年十二月的一個寒冷的日子裡，他們到達第一個人類成功飛行的紀錄。這

就是為什麼如果我可以當一個留名歷史的人，我要選擇當萊特兄弟之一的理由。他們追求夢想的勇氣，產生了一個改變世界的發明，並且使人類希望像鳥類一樣飛翔的夢想，得以實現。

 **Vocabulary**

topic	話題；標題
envy	忌妒；羨慕
ability	能力
symbolize	象徵
mankind	人類
flight	飛行
drop out	輟學
regular	尋常的；規律的；常態的
experiment	實驗
object	物體；實體
support	支持；支援

courage	勇氣

 **Useful Sentences**

◎ A pair of 一對

two of something
(*example: a pair of shoes, a pair of brothers*)
兩個東西（例如：一雙鞋子；一對兄弟）

A: Are you sure that you know the rules of this card game?
你確定你知道玩牌的規則？

B: Yes, to win I must put down a pair of twos, threes, or fours.
是的，我必須出一對二、三或四才能贏。

◎ A dream come true 美夢成真

used to say that something really good that is unlikely to happen, has actually happened
指好的令人不敢相信的事，真的發生了

A: You are so lucky! You have a BMW, a huge apartment, and you no longer have to work!
你真是太幸運了！擁有一輛 BMW、一棟大公寓，而且再也不用工作了。

B: Yes, winning the lottery really was a dream come true.

是啊，中了樂透真是美夢成真哪。

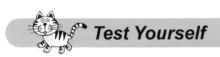 **Test Yourself**

1. If Eric could be any person in history, who would he like to be?

   A) a bird

   B) Orville Wright

   C) Wilbur Wright

   D) one of the Wright brothers

2. What does Eric admire about the Wright brothers?

   A) They were wrong about flight.

   B) They were the first humans to fly.

   C) They dropped out of high school.

   D) They lived long ago.

3. What contributed to the Wright brothers' success?

   A) their parent's support

   B) their courage

C) their intelligence

D) all of the above

---

4. When was the first human flight?

    A) thousands of years ago

    B) in Leonardo da Vinci's day

    C) just over one hundred years ago

    D) last December

---

5. What do Eric and the Wright brothers have in common?

    A) They are all poor students.

    B) They are all stupid.

    C) They all are in the same class.

    D) They all know how to fly.

測驗題庫中譯

1. 如果艾瑞克可以成為留名歷史的人，他想成為誰？

    A) 一隻鳥　　　　　　　　　B) 歐維爾‧萊特

    C) 威爾伯‧萊特　　　　　　D) 萊特兄弟其中一個

2. 艾瑞克欣賞萊特兄弟哪一點？

    A) 他們對於飛行的錯誤　　　B) 他們是第一對飛行的人類

    C) 他們從中學輟學　　　　　D) 他們生活在很久以前

3. 是什麼導致了萊特兄弟的成功？

    A) 他們父母的支持　　　　　B) 他們的勇氣

    C) 他們的聰明才智　　　　　D) 以上皆是

4. 何時是人類的第一次飛行？

    A) 幾千年前　　　　　　　　B) 李奧納多‧達文西的時代

    C) 一百多年前　　　　　　　D) 去年十二月

5. 艾瑞克和萊特兄弟有什麼共通之處？

    A) 他們都是成績不好的學生　B) 他們都很笨

    C) 他們在同一個班級　　　　D) 他們都知道怎麼飛行

Unit 4 Lunchtime

***The bell has rung, and Eric has gone to
speak to Miss Jones.***

Eric :	You wanted to speak to me, Miss Jones?
Miss Jones :	Yes, Eric.
Eric :	Is it about my assignment? I'll work harder next time, I promise...
Miss Jones :	No, it's not that. In fact, I glanced over your assignment after I asked the class to do some group work. It looks pretty good!
Eric :	Really? What a relief!
Miss Jones :	But that's not what I wanted to talk to you about. I wanted to ask you why you seem to be having trouble concentrating lately?
Eric :	Er...umm...
Miss Jones :	Do you have any idea why? You keep daydreaming, Eric.
Eric :	I'm sorry.
Miss Jones :	I've written a note that I'd like you to give to your mother. Would you please

take it to her for me, and bring back a reply?

Eric : Um, OK Miss Jones.

Miss Jones : Here it is. Please don't forget to give it to her. I'll be expecting a reply tomorrow.

Eric is in the schoolyard about to eat his lunch when Kimberly sees him and comes over.

Kimberly : Mind if I join you?

Eric : Not at all.

Kimberly : (unpacking her lunch) Ugh! Another peanut butter sandwich. My mom puts one in my lunch every day. What do you have?

Eric : A ham sandwich. Do you want it?

Kimberly : Aren't you going to eat it?

Eric : No, I'm not hungry.

Kimberly : That's not like you at all! Normally you eat more than anyone else I know!

Eric : I don't have much of an appetite today.

Kimberly asks Eric what's wrong.

Kimberly :	Does it have something to do with your meeting with Miss Jones? Was she unhappy with your assignment?
Eric :	No, she likes my assignment, I think. But she thinks I'm not doing a good job of concentrating in class.
Kimberly :	Oh. Is she giving you detention?
Eric :	No, no detention. But she wrote a letter, and she wants me to give it to my mother!
Kimberly :	Really? What does the letter say?
Eric :	I don't know. I haven't read it--- it's for my mother.
Kimberly :	I think that you should read it. Then you can decide whether or not to give it to her. If it's something really bad, your mother might punish you. Didn't she say once that if your grades didn't improve, you'd have to quit the baseball team?
Eric :	You're right. OK, let's read it.

午餐時間

鐘聲響了，艾瑞克去找瓊斯小姐談話。

艾瑞克： 瓊斯小姐，妳有話要對我說？

瓊斯小姐： 是的，艾瑞克。

艾瑞克： 有關我的作業嗎？我下次會更努力的，我保證……

瓊斯小姐： 不，不是這件事情。事實上，我要學生們做小組討論的時候瞄了一下你的作業，看起來相當好。

艾瑞克： 真的嗎？真是鬆了一口氣！

瓊斯小姐： 不過那不是我找你來的原因。我想問你為什麼最近似乎都不太專心呢？

艾瑞克： 這個……嗯……

瓊斯小姐： 你可以解釋為什麼嗎？艾瑞克，你老是在做白日夢。

艾瑞克： 我很抱歉。

瓊斯小姐： 我已經寫了一張字條，我希望你拿給你媽媽看。你願意幫我拿給她，然後給我你媽媽的回函嗎？

艾瑞克： 嗯，好的，瓊斯小姐。

瓊斯小姐： 在這裡。不要忘記拿給她。我很期待明天的回條。

艾瑞克在校園裡正要吃午餐，金柏莉看到他然後走過來。

金柏莉： 介意我跟你一起吃嗎？

艾瑞克： 一點也不。

金柏莉： （打開她的午餐盒）噁，又是花生奶油三明治。我媽媽每天都做這個給我當午餐。你吃什麼？

艾瑞克： 火腿三明治。你想吃嗎？

金柏莉： 你不吃嗎？

艾瑞克： 不，我不餓。

金柏莉： 這一點都不像你。就我所知，你可是個大胃王呢。

艾瑞克： 我今天沒什麼食慾。

金柏莉詢問艾瑞克怎麼了。

金柏莉： 和你跟瓊斯小姐的面談有關嗎？她不滿意你的作業嗎？

艾瑞克： 不是，我想她很喜歡我的作業，但她覺得我在上課時不太專心。

金柏莉： 喔，她要你留校察看嗎？

艾瑞克： 沒有，不用留校。但她寫了封信，要我拿給我媽媽。

金柏莉： 真的嗎？信上說什麼？

艾瑞克： 我不知道。我還沒看，那是給我媽媽的。

金柏莉： 我想你應該看的。這樣你才能決定是不是要給你媽媽看。如果真的是很嚴重的事情，你媽媽可能會處罰你。她不是說過要是你的成績都沒有進步，你就得退出棒球隊嗎？

艾瑞克： 沒錯。好吧，我們看看吧。

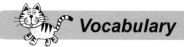 *Vocabulary*

lunchtime	午餐時間
promise	保證
glance over	瞥一眼；略看
have trouble doing something	做某事有困難
concentrate	專心
daydream	白日夢
reply	回答；回信；回應
expect	期待
mind	介意
unpack	打開；拆開
peanut butter	花生奶油
appetite	食慾
detention	延遲；留滯
punish	處罰

improve	進步
quit	放棄

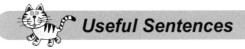 **Useful Sentences**

◎ Not at all　**一點也不**

used to express "no" in a strong way

用以表示強烈的否定

A: Do you like our teacher?
　　你喜歡我們的老師嗎？

B: Not at all. She isn't very good at explaining the things we're learning in class.
　　一點也不。課堂上的東西她總是解釋得不清不楚。

◎ Normally　**平常**

usually

通常

A: I normally don't eat at fast food restaurants.
　　我通常不到速食店吃東西。

B: That's a good habit. Fast food isn't very healthy.
　　那是個好習慣。速食都不太健康。

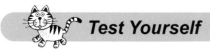

Test Yourself

1. Why doesn't Eric feel like eating?

    A) He has a big appetite.

    B) He doesn't like ham sandwiches.

    C) He feels too unhappy to eat.

    D) He ate too much food at breakfast.

2. What did Miss Jones discuss with Eric?

    A) his poorly written assignment

    B) his excellent grades

    C) his popularity

    D) his behavior in class

3. What does Miss Jones give to Eric?

    A) a note for his mother

    B) detention after class

    C) another lunch to eat

    D) another assignment to write

4. What might Eric's mother do if his grades don't improve?

    A) make him quit baseball

    B) make him quit summer school

    C) give him a reward

    D) stop making him lunch

5. What does Eric decide to do with the letter?

    A) throw it away   B) give it to his mother

    C) read it   D) forget about it

 測驗題庫中譯

1. 為什麼艾瑞克不想吃東西？

    A) 他食量很大   B) 他不喜歡火腿三明治

    C) 他難過得吃不下   D) 他早餐吃太多了

2. 瓊斯小姐跟艾瑞克討論什麼事情？

    A) 他的作業寫得不好   B) 他優異的成績

    C) 他的人緣   D) 他上課的表現

3. 瓊斯小姐給艾瑞克什麼東西？

    A) 一張給他媽媽的紙條   B) 留校察看

C) 給他另一份午餐吃   D) 給他寫另一份作業

4. 如果艾瑞克的成績沒有進步，他媽媽可能會怎樣？

A) 要他退出棒球隊   B) 不讓他上暑期課程

C) 給他獎勵   D) 不做午餐給他吃

5. 艾瑞克決定要怎麼處理這封信？

A) 把它丟掉   B) 給他媽媽

C) 偷讀   D) 忘記它

Unit 5 — A Note from School

Dear Mrs. Lin,

I am writing about your son, Eric, who I am teaching this summer at school. Eric is a bright student, and I have been impressed with the assignments he has turned in. His homework is always complete, and I can see that he is improving in this regard.

However, I have noticed that Eric has been experiencing difficulties concentrating in class. On a number of occasions he has been daydreaming when he should be listening to a lecture or doing work. I am worried that if this behavior continues, Eric's grades will fall. And if this happens, then I am afraid he will not pass his summer classes. He will have to repeat grade ten next year, instead of moving on to the eleventh grade with his classmates.

I think that it would be in Eric's best interest if we could meet face to face to discuss this situation. I hope that if I know more, I can help Eric to perform better in school.

Sincerely,
Hannah Jones

給家長的信

親愛的林太太：

我寫這信是要談談您的兒子艾瑞克，我是他的暑期輔導老師。艾瑞克是個聰明的學生，而我也對於他交的作業感到印象深刻。從不缺交作業，我也看得出來在這方面他進步很多。

然而，我注意到艾瑞克在課堂上一直很難專心。有好幾次，他應該要聽講或者做練習時，他卻像在做白日夢的樣子。我很擔心這個情況如果持續下去，艾瑞克的成績會一落千丈。這樣的話，暑期課程恐怕就無法通過。那他明年就得留級，而無法和他的同學繼續升上十一年級了。

我想跟您面對面談一談這個情況，對艾瑞克是最好的。希望可以對艾瑞克多了解一點，才能幫助他在學校表現得更好。

您真誠的

漢娜・瓊斯

 **Vocabulary**

bright	明亮的；聰明的
impress	使印象深刻
turn in	遞交

complete	完成；完整的
difficulty	困難
occasion	情況；場合
lecture	演講；講課
repeat	重複
perform	表現；表演

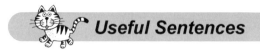 **Useful Sentences**

◎ In this / that regard　就這 / 那點而言

in this/that way
在這 / 那方面而言

A: This house is a little too far away from the kids' school. I'm not sure we should buy it.
這個房子距離孩子的學校有點太遠了。我不確定是否應該買下來。

B: But the price is good and in this regard, I think it's the right place for us.
可是價格很好，就這點而言，我覺得這就是我們要的地方。

◎ In somebody's best interest 某人的最大利益

used to say that something is done because it is the best thing for somebody
說明這麼做對某人來說是最好的

A: So, you're not going to the movies with us tonight?
那麼，你今晚不和我們去看電影囉？

B: No. It's in my best interest to stay home and study for the test.
不。留在家裡讀書準備考試，對我而言是最好的選擇。

◎ Face to face 面對面

used to say that one will meet somebody to talk about something directly
指面對面談論事情

A: This phone connection is bad. I can hardly understand you!
這支電話線壞掉了。我很難聽得懂你說什麼。

B: Why don't we meet at the coffee shop? It will be easier to talk face to face.
何不在咖啡館見個面呢？面對面談話容易多了。

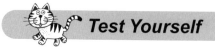 **Test Yourself**

1. What does Miss Jones think of Eric?
   A) He is stupid.　　　　B) He is quite smart.
   C) He is lazy.　　　　　D) He is perfect.

2. In what way has Eric become a better student?
   A) He does a good job on his homework.
   B) He pays attention in class.
   C) He is improving his grades.
   D) He has a lot of friends.

3. When Eric should be listening, what does he do instead?
   A) He chats with his friends.
   B) He falls asleep.
   C) He daydreams.
   D) He argues with the teacher.

4. What will happen if Eric doesn't start paying attention?
   A) He will go to grade eleven.
   B) He will stay in grade ten.

C) He will stay in summer school.

D) He will pass all of his classes.

5. What does Miss Jones want to do?

A) see Eric fail

B) punish Eric

C) make Eric leave

D) talk to Eric's mother

 測驗題庫中譯

1. 瓊斯小姐對艾瑞克有什麼感覺？

   A) 他很笨   B) 他相當聰明

   C) 他很懶惰   D) 他很完美

2. 艾瑞克在哪方面有進步？

   A) 他的回家功課寫得很好   B) 他上課專心

   C) 他的成績有進步   D) 他有很多朋友

3. 當艾瑞克應該聽講時，他反而在做什麼呢？

   A) 他和他的朋友聊天   B) 他睡著了

   C) 做白日夢   D) 他和老師爭辯

4. 要是艾瑞克再不專心上課，會發生什麼事情？

A) 他將升上十一年級　　　　B) 他要留級

C) 他得留在暑期學校　　　　D) 他會通過所有的課程

5. 瓊斯小姐希望做什麼？

A) 看到艾瑞克失敗　　　　B) 處罰艾瑞克

C) 讓艾瑞克離開　　　　D) 和艾瑞克的媽媽談談

Unit 6 Eric's Plan

Eric has finished reading the letter out loud to Kimberly.

Kimberly : Oh my goodness! What are you going to do?

Eric : What can I do? I've got to give the note to my mom.

Kimberly : Says who?

Eric : Miss Jones! She wants me to bring a reply to her tomorrow and now I know why! She wants to talk to my mom in person.

Kimberly : Listen, I have an idea.

Eric : I'm all ears.

Kimberly : I can write a reply for you. I'll disguise my handwriting—Miss Jones will never know!

Eric : What would you write in the note?

Kimberly : Nothing much, just something polite, like "Thank you for your concern."

Eric : But what about the meeting?

Kimberly : I'd write "Sorry, but I'm too busy these days."

Eric :   Kim, you're terrible!

Kimberly :   So you don't want to give it a try?

Eric :   Far from it! Have you got a pen? Let's write it!

Later on, Eric goes home. He is in his bedroom listening to music when his mother knocks on the door.

Eric :   Come in!

Aunt June : Hey, kiddo. How was school today?

Eric :   Um... good.

Aunt June : You handed in your assignment?

Eric :   Yep.

Aunt June : Did anything interesting happen? Anything you want to talk about?

Eric :   No. Why do you keep asking me?

Aunt June : I just want to make sure everything is OK...

Eric :   It is. Now can I just listen to my music please? I feel like being alone.

Aunt June : OK. Just so you know, dinner will be ready in half an hour.

艾瑞克的計劃

艾瑞克已經把信念出來給金柏莉聽了。

金柏莉： 天哪！你要怎麼做？

艾瑞克： 我能怎麼辦？我得把信交給我媽媽。

金柏莉： 誰說的？

艾瑞克： 瓊斯小姐。她要我明天帶回條給她，現在我知道為什麼了。她想要親自跟我媽媽談談。

金柏莉： 聽著，我有個主意。

艾瑞克： 我洗耳恭聽。

金柏莉： 我可以幫你寫一張回條。我會偽裝筆跡，瓊斯小姐不會知道的。

艾瑞克： 你要在字條裡寫什麼呢？

金柏莉： 一些禮貌性的回覆就好，比如：「謝謝您的關心」。

艾瑞克： 可是會談怎麼辦？

金柏莉： 我就寫：「抱歉，我最近太忙了。」

艾瑞克： 金，你好惡劣。

金柏莉： 那麼你不願意嘗試囉？

艾瑞克： 當然不是！你有筆嗎？我們來寫吧。

一會兒之後，艾瑞克回家了。當他在自己房間聽音樂，他媽媽來敲門。

艾瑞克： 請進！

茱兒阿姨： 嘿，孩子，今天在學校怎麼樣啊？

艾瑞克： 　嗯，很好啊。

茱兒阿姨：你的作業交了嗎？

艾瑞克： 　交了！

茱兒阿姨：有什麼有趣的事情嗎？你想告訴我什麼嗎？

艾瑞克： 　沒有。你為什麼這樣問？

茱兒阿姨：我只是想確定一切都很好……

艾瑞克： 　都很好啊。現在我只想聽音樂可以嗎？我想要獨處。

茱兒阿姨：好。我只是要讓你知道，晚餐在半小時後就好了。

 **Vocabulary**

reply	回信；回應
disguise	喬裝；偽裝；掩飾
handwriting	筆跡
polite	禮貌的
concern	關心；擔憂
terrible	糟糕的；令人敬畏的；嚇人的
kiddo	孩子（親暱的稱呼）
alone	獨自的

Useful Sentences

◎ Out loud **大聲說**

said in such a way that everyone can hear you
用每個人都能聽見的音量說話

A: There is a funny story in the newspaper! You should come take a look!
報紙上有一則有趣的故事。你應該過來看看。

B: I'm busy washing the dishes. Why don't you read it out loud to me?
我在忙著洗碗盤。你為什麼不大聲念出來給我聽呢？

◎ In person **親自**

done in the presence of somebody else
在別人面前出現

A: Do you want to come down to the mall with me? Brad Pitt is scheduled to be there signing his autograph!
你要跟我一起去購物中心嗎？布萊德・彼特要到那兒辦簽名會。

B: Brad Pitt will be there in person? Of course I'll come along- I'd love to see him.
布萊德・彼特本人？我當然要去──我想見他。

◎ Be all ears 洗耳恭聽

to listen carefully; be very interested or ready to listen
仔細聽；興致勃勃地來聽

A: Did you hear what the teacher said about the field trip?
你有聽到老師説戶外教學的事嗎？

B: No, I must have been in the bathroom at the time. Can you tell me? I'm all ears!
沒有，我那時一定是去廁所了。你可以告訴我嗎？我想聽。

◎ Give something a try 嘗試某事情

to try something
試著做某事

A: I've never been skiing before. It looks scary to go down a hill like that!
我以前從未滑過雪。從山丘上滑下去看起來好可怕！

B: It's not really. You should come with me. You'll never know what skiing is like unless you give it a try!
沒那麼可怕。你應該跟我去滑雪的。除非你試過，不然你無法體會滑雪的樂趣。

◎ Far from it 差遠了

the reality being very different from what has just been said
意指事實與剛剛所說的相差甚遠

A: Are all the dishes done?
　　碗盤都洗好了嗎？

B: Far from it! There are plenty more left to wash.
　　還早呢。還有很多沒有洗。

◎ Make sure 確定

to check and be certain of something
確認且確定某事

A: Did you remember to turn out all of the lights and lock the door?
　　你有記得把所有的燈關掉，把門鎖上嗎？

B: I think so--- but if you'll wait a moment, I'll go back and make sure.
　　我想我有……不過如果你願意等一下，我就回去確認。

 **Test Yourself**

1. What does Eric decide to do with Miss Jones's note?

    A) not to give it to his mother

    B) to give it to his mother

    C) to give it back to Miss Jones

    D) to share it with his whole family

2. Who will write the reply to Miss Jones?

    A) Eric   B) Kimberly

    C) Aunt June   D) Miss Jones

3. What will the note not say?

    A) that Aunt June will meet Miss Jones in person

    B) that Aunt June appreciates Miss Jones's concern

    C) that Aunt June is very busy these days

    D) that Aunt June thanks Miss Jones

4. What does Eric do when he gets home from school?

    A) He gives his mother the note.

    B) He listens to music in his room.

    C) He argues with his mother.

    D) He writes a note to Miss Jones.

5. What can we say about Eric's mother?

A) She is not worried about Eric.

B) She wants to listen to music with Eric.

C) She is more interested in dinner than in Eric.

D) She is curious about his day at school.

 測驗題庫中譯

1. 艾瑞克決定怎麼處理瓊斯小姐的信？

A) 不給他媽媽　　B) 給他媽媽

C) 拿回去給瓊斯小姐　　　　D) 跟他的家人分享

2. 誰要寫回信給瓊斯小姐？

A) 艾瑞克　　　B) 金柏莉

C) 茱兒阿姨　　D) 瓊斯小姐

3. 信上將不會寫什麼？

A) 茱兒阿姨將親自和瓊斯小姐面談

B) 茱兒阿姨很感謝瓊斯小姐的關心

C) 茱兒阿姨最近很忙

D) 茱兒阿姨很謝謝瓊斯小姐

4. 當艾瑞克從學校回到家裡時，他做什麼事？

    A) 他把信給他媽媽   B) 他在房間聽音樂

    C) 他和媽媽爭辯   D) 他寫一封信給瓊斯小姐

5. 我們可以怎麼形容艾瑞克的媽媽？

    A) 她不擔心艾瑞克

    B) 她想和艾瑞克一起聽音樂

    C) 她對晚餐的興趣大於對艾瑞克的興趣

    D) 她對於他在學校的生活很好奇

Unit 7 Eric's Choices

After Aunt June left his room, Eric felt terrible. He knew his mom only meant the best, and would help him no matter what— but he just couldn't bring himself to tell her he was having problems at school.

At dinner, Eric was quiet, and acted unlike himself. He didn't help himself to seconds, and he said that he wasn't in the mood for dessert. When he helped his mother clear the table after dinner, she asked him again if anything was wrong. This time he decided to tell her the whole truth.

He said that Miss Jones had written a note asking to meet Aunt June to discuss the difficulties Eric was having at school. Then Eric said that he had been too worried to tell her because he thought it might mean that he'd have to give up baseball.

Aunt June's feelings were mixed. She was unhappy that Eric wasn't doing well in school. But she was happy that he had worked up the courage to tell her. She told him not to worry — she would meet with Miss Jones, and try to understand Eric's problem. Only then could they all work together to find a solution and, if all went well, it would mean that Eric needn't give up baseball.

Then Uncle George interrupted. He was angry. Not because Eric's grades were poor, or because the teacher wanted to meet with Aunt June. But because he had found the note Kimberly and Eric had written and signed with Aunt June's name. It had fallen out of Eric's pocket. Uncle George was upset that Eric would forge a letter. He said it meant that Eric couldn't be trusted.

Uncle George grounded Eric. He said he could still play baseball, but that he wasn't allowed to hang out with his friends — especially Kimberly. Eric felt very sorry, but knew that his father was right.

艾瑞克的選擇

　　茱兒阿姨離開艾瑞克的房間後,他覺得糟透了。他知道他媽媽完全是好意,而且不管怎樣都會幫助他的——但,他就是無法讓她知道他在學校有問題。

晚餐時，艾瑞克很安靜，跟平常不一樣。他說他沒有心情吃甜點。當他在晚餐後幫忙媽媽清理桌子時，她又問了他一次是否有什麼事情不對勁。這一次，他決定要告訴她整個實話。

他說瓊斯小姐寫了一封信，表示要和茱兒阿姨討論艾瑞克在學校遇到的瓶頸。然後艾瑞克說，他一直很擔心所以不想告訴她，因為他認為這也許意謂著，他必須退出棒球隊。

茱兒阿姨的感覺很複雜。艾瑞克在學校表現不好，讓她很傷心，但他提起勇氣告訴她實話，讓她覺得很高興。她對他說別太擔心，她會和瓊斯小姐見面，並且試著去了解艾瑞克的困難之處。只有這樣他們才能一起合作找出解決之道，如果一切都進行順利，艾瑞克就不用退出棒球隊了。

喬治姨丈打斷了他們。他很生氣。這不是因為艾瑞克的成績不好，也不是因為老師想跟茱兒阿姨見面，而是因為他發現了金柏莉和艾瑞克寫好的回信，上面簽了茱兒阿姨的名字。信從艾瑞克的口袋掉出來，喬治姨丈非常氣惱艾瑞克會偽造文書，他說這意謂著艾瑞克不是值得信賴的人。

喬治姨丈禁足了艾瑞克。他說他可以繼續打棒球，但他不准和他的朋友出去玩，特別是金柏莉。艾瑞克感到很抱歉，但他知道他的父親是對的。

 *Vocabulary*

terrible	糟糕的
solution	解決之道
give up	放棄
interrupt	打斷
fall out of	掉出來
forge	偽造；編造
trust	信任
ground	禁足
hang out with	出去閒晃；鬼混

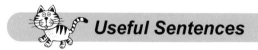

Useful Sentences

◎ No matter what **不管怎樣**

under any circumstances
在任何情況下

A: Will you love me, even if I am old, or sick, or poor?
即使我老了、病了、或者很窮,你還是愛我嗎?

B: Honey, you don't need to worry. I'll love you no matter what!
親愛的,你不用擔心。不管怎樣我都會愛你的。

◎ Have mixed feelings **感覺複雜**

to feel several different things about something
對某事懷有多種不同的感覺

A: How do you feel about the speech competition?
你對於演講比賽有什麼感覺?

B: I have mixed feelings about it. I'm excited because I think my speech has a chance of winning. But I'm also very nervous.
感覺很複雜。我很興奮,因為我覺得我有機會贏,但我也非常緊張。

◎ Work up **激發**

to muster; to gather
鼓起；集結

A: Ready to go swimming, yet?
    準備好要游泳了嗎？

B: Not yet! I haven't worked up the nerve to jump into such cold water!
    還沒！我膽子還不夠跳進這麼冰冷的水裡！

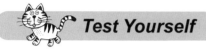 **Test Yourself**

1. How did Eric feel after his mother left the room?

   A) His feelings were mixed.   B) He felt confident.

   C) He felt really bad.   D) He felt hungry.

2. What was unusual about the way Eric acted at
   dinner?

   A) He ate like a pig.   B) He hardly ate anything.

   C) He had two desserts.   D) He wanted lots to eat.

3. When did Eric tell his mother the truth?

   A) while they were eating dinner

   B) while they were cleaning up

   C) while they were talking to Uncle George

   D) while he was writing a note

4. Why was Uncle George angry?

   A) because Eric was a poor student

   B) because Eric didn't eat his dinner

   C) because Eric cheated on a test

   D) because Eric forged a note

5. What did Uncle George do to Eric?

    A) He punished him.   B) He congratulated him.

    C) He celebrated with him.   D) He promoted him.

測驗題庫中譯

1. 當艾瑞克的媽媽離開房間時,他有什麼感覺?

    A) 他感覺很複雜   B) 他感覺很有信心

    C) 他覺得很糟   D) 他覺得很餓

2. 晚餐時艾瑞克有什麼不尋常?

    A) 他吃得像隻豬   B) 他幾乎沒吃什麼東西

    C) 他吃了兩份甜點   D) 他想要吃很多東西

3. 什麼時候艾瑞克告訴他媽媽實情?

    A) 在他們吃晚餐時   B) 在他們清理東西時

    C) 在他們跟喬治姨丈說話時   D) 在他寫信的時候

4. 喬治姨丈為什麼生氣?

    A) 因為艾瑞克的成績很差   B) 因為艾瑞克沒有吃晚餐

    C) 因為艾瑞克考試作弊   D) 因為艾瑞克假造信件

5. 喬治姨丈怎麼處理艾瑞克的事?

    A) 他處罰了他   B) 他恭喜他

    C) 他和他一起慶祝   D) 他表揚他

Chapter ③ Uncle George's Day
喬治叔叔的一天

Unit 1 Uncle George

Uncle George is forty years old. He works at an advertising agency. His job requires a lot of creative thinking — and you will see that Uncle George has quite an active imagination.

Uncle George didn't always work in advertising. He was once a writer. In university, he worked on the student newspaper. He took creative writing courses. He dreamed of being a famous writer and writing many novels, but things didn't quite work out the way he had dreamed they would. He did get a job at a newspaper when he graduated — but working as an assistant in the advertising department. His job was to talk to advertisers about the ads they wanted to run in the paper.

Usually the ads were very dull. One time, a company wanted to run an ad for its product. The company had already decided what the ad should say, but Uncle George had a better idea. He thought the ad could be much more exciting. The company loved this idea, and asked him to print the ad like that.

Over the next year, things like this happened often,

and it occurred to Uncle George that maybe he had a talent for advertising. So he decided to take a risk. He quit his job at the newspaper, and started his own advertising company... and the rest is history!

For the last fifteen years, Uncle George's company has done very well. His company is very successful. They have accounts for many different kinds of companies and have ads on the TV, the radio, and in many newspapers. Uncle George loves his job — especially since he's the owner. That means he can take time off when he needs to — to work on his novel!

喬治姨丈

喬治姨丈今年四十歲。他在一家廣告公司工作。他的工作需要很多創意思考，而你會發現喬治姨丈擁有相當活躍的想像力。

喬治姨丈並不是一直在做廣告工作。他曾經是個作家。大學時，他為一家學生報社工作。他修習創意寫作的課程，夢想成為一個有名的作家，並且寫出許多小說。但是事情並不如他夢想的那樣進行。他畢業後確實得到了一份在報社的工作，不過是在廣告部門當助理。他的工作是和廣告商談論他們想要登在報紙上的廣告。

通常這些廣告都非常無聊拙劣。有一次，一家公司想為他們的產品登廣告，這家公司已經決定這則廣告要寫些什麼了，但是喬治姨丈有個更好的點子。他認為這個廣告應該要更具刺激性。這家公司愛極他的點子，並決定依照他的建議刊登廣告。

隔年，類似的事情發生了好多次，這激發了喬治姨丈，他想他也許有廣告天份，因此他決定要冒險一試。他辭掉了在報社的工作，並經營他自己的廣告公司……接下來的事大家都知道了。

這十五年來，喬治姨丈的公司運作得非常好，他相當成功。他們擁有許多不同種類的客戶，並且在電視、廣播以及許多報紙上都有刊登廣告。喬治姨丈熱愛他的工作，特別是當他成為老闆以後，因為當他想寫小說時，他就可以隨時休假了。

Vocabulary

advertising agency	廣告公司
require	需要
creative	有創意的
active	活躍的；活潑的
imagination	想像力

graduate	畢業
assistant	助理
run something in a paper	在報紙上刊登某事
dull	無趣的；遲鈍拙劣的
print	刊印
account	生意往來
time off	休息

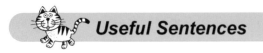

Useful Sentences

◎ Turn out **演變**

the result
結果

A: How did your history exam turn out?
你的歷史考試結果怎樣？

B: Well, it was pretty difficult... but I got an A!
這個嘛，考試很難…不過我拿了 A。

◎ The rest is history **結果大家都知道**

used to say that the result of something that happened in the past is obvious or well known
用以說明發生在過去的某事，其結果是明顯的或者眾所皆知

A: In 1492, Columbus sailed across the Atlantic Ocean.
1492 年時，哥倫比亞航海跨過大西洋。

B: That's right. He discovered America... and the rest is history!
沒錯。他發現了美洲……後來的事就眾所皆知了。

 **Review Questions**

1. How old is Uncle George?

    A) thirty   B) forty

    C) fifty   D) sixty

2. What did Uncle George do in university?

    A) He wrote a novel.

    B) He started an advertising agency.

    C) He worked on a newspaper.

    D) He was an assistant in the advertising department.

3. What can we say about Uncle George?

    A) He is a failure.   B) He hates his job.

    C) He has no talent.   D) He is creative.

4. How long has Uncle George owned his company?

    A) five years   B) ten years

    C) fifteen years   D) twenty years

5. What does Uncle George take time off to do?

    A) Write a book.   B) Work at a newspaper.

    C) Go to college.   D) Start a company.

 測驗題庫中譯

1. 喬治姨丈幾歲？
    A) 三十   B) 四十   C) 五十   D) 六十

2. 喬治姨丈在大學時做什麼？
    A) 他寫小說   B) 他開了一家廣告公司

    C) 他在報社工作   D) 他是廣告部門的助理

3. 我們可以怎麼形容喬治姨丈？
    A) 他是個失敗者   B) 他恨他的工作

    C) 他沒有天份   D) 他很有創意

4. 喬治姨丈經營他的公司多久了？
    A) 五年   B) 十年

    C) 十五年   D) 二十年

5. 喬治姨丈休假時做什麼事情？
    A) 寫書   B) 在報社工作

    C) 上大學   D) 開公司

Unit 2 Uncle George at Work

Today Uncle George arrived at work, early as usual. He greeted all of his employees and put his lunch bag in the refrigerator in the employee lounge. He put the bag at the back of the fridge, and sighed. He was pretty sure there would be another mix up with his lunch today.

Every day now, for a week, some mistake had been made at lunchtime when the employees were getting their food from the fridge. One day, Mr. Robbins had accidentally taken Uncle George's bag instead of his own, and eaten his tuna salad sandwich. Another day, Miss Jenkins had mistaken his lunch bag for garbage when she was cleaning out the fridge! Both days, Uncle George had gone home hungry, and in a bad mood!

It reminded him a lot of his university days, when he lived in an apartment he shared with four other students. Back then, Uncle George had had a problem with his roommates sneaking his food when he wasn't looking. Once, after visiting his mother, he had come back to the apartment with some of her baking. Within a few hours, it had all been eaten! Uncle George had been furious, and decided to take action.

The next time he went to his mother's, he came back with some sandwiches that he had made himself. He left them on a plate in the kitchen, and sure enough, they disappeared within a couple of hours. To this day, he'll never forget the looks on everybody's faces when he innocently asked what had happened to his cat food sandwiches!

Unfortunately, Uncle George cannot play a trick like that at work. But if he could, he'd definitely have enough to eat every day at lunch!

工作中的喬治姨丈

今天喬治姨丈跟平常一樣早到公司，他和所有員工打招呼後，把他的午餐袋放進員工休息室的冰箱裡。他把袋子放到冰箱的後層，嘆了口氣。他非常確定今天一定又會有另一個便當跟他的午餐混淆。

　一整個禮拜當中，每天的午餐時間，當員工們從冰箱拿出他們的食物時，總會發生一些錯誤。有一天，羅賓斯先生不小心拿了喬治姨丈的袋子，並且吃掉了他的鮪魚沙拉三明治。又有一天，珍金絲小姐在清理冰箱的時候，把他的午餐袋誤認為是垃圾。這兩天裡，喬治姨丈都餓著肚子回家，而且心情相當不好。

　這些事情讓他想起了大學裡的許多日子，那時他跟另外四個學生合租一層公寓。回想當時，喬治姨丈的室友們會趁他不注意時，偷吃他的食物，這讓他相當困擾。曾經有一次，在他去看他的母親後，他帶著媽媽給的烤食回到公寓。幾個小時後，那些烤食全被吃光了。喬治姨丈感到很憤怒，他決定要採取行動。

　下一次當他又去看他媽媽時，他帶回一些他自己做的三明治。他把它們放在廚房的一個盤子上，而且相當確定它們在幾個小時內會消失無蹤。他永遠也無法忘記，當他天真地問起他的貓食三明治怎麼不見時，每個人臉上的表情。

　可是，喬治姨丈無法在工作時這樣惡作劇。如果可以的話，他每天午餐絕對會吃得飽飽的。

Vocabulary

greet	打招呼
lounge	休息室；大廳
sigh	嘆氣
mix up	搞混；混淆
accidentally	意外地；無意中
tuna salad	鮪魚沙拉
mistaken	誤會；弄錯
remind	提醒
share	分享
baking	烤的食物
furious	生氣的；憤怒的
take action	採取行動
plate	盤子
innocently	純潔地；天真地

cat food	貓食
trick	詭計；騙局；惡作劇
definitely	絕對地

 Useful Sentences

◎ As usual　**如同往常**

used to say that something happens as it normally does
用以說明某事的發生如同平時一樣

A: Debbie was late catching the bus for school, as usual.
黛比如同往常一樣，沒趕上上學的公車。

B: That girl has got to learn to be more responsible!
那個女孩要學著更有責任感些。

◎ In a good / bad mood　**處於好 / 壞心情**

used to say that somebody is happy / not happy
用以說明某人很快樂 / 不快樂

A: You look like you're in a good mood today! You've got a huge smile on your face!
你今天看起來心情很好。你臉上一直掛著大大的笑容。

B: I know! I just learned that I got accepted into a great university!
沒錯。我剛剛知道我申請到一所很棒的大學。

 **Review Questions**

1. When did Uncle George get to work?

    A) early   B) on time

    C) late   D) never

2. What did he do after he said hello to his employees?

    A) He played a trick on them.

    B) He went to school.

    C) He put his lunch in the fridge.

    D) He ate a sandwich.

3. What had put Uncle George in a bad mood lately?

    A) He never got to eat his lunch.

    B) He missed his college roommates.

    C) He had fired his employees.

D) He didn't enjoy his job.

4. In university, what kind of sandwich did Uncle
   George make?
   A) tuna salad   B) peanut butter
   C) ham   D) cat food

5. Why did Uncle George play a trick on his roommates in
   college?
   A) They accidentally threw out his food when they cleaned
      out the fridge.
   B) They mistook his lunch bag for theirs.
   C) They always shared their food with him.
   D) They ate his food and left him with none.

 測驗題庫中譯

1. 喬治姨丈什麼時候去上班？
    A) 很早   B) 準時

    C) 遲到   D) 從不上班

2. 在他跟員工打過招呼後，他做了什麼事情？
    A) 他對他們惡作劇   B) 他去上學

    C) 他把午餐放在冰箱裡面   D) 他吃了一個三明治

3. 最近什麼事情讓喬治姨丈心情不好？
    A) 他沒吃到午餐   B) 他想念他的大學室友

    C) 他開除他的員工   D) 他不喜歡他的工作

4. 大學時代，喬治姨丈曾做了哪種三明治？
    A) 鮪魚三明治   B) 花生奶油

    C) 火腿   D) 貓食

5. 為什麼喬治姨丈要對他的大學室友惡作劇呢？
    A) 他們清理冰箱時，不小心把他的食物丟掉了

    B) 他們拿錯他的午餐袋

    C) 他們總是與他分享食物

    D) 他們把他的食物吃光

Unit 3 Uncle George's Email Account

To: George@creativecodes.com
Sender: Mike@commacola.com
Subject: Urgent help needed!

Hello George,

Long time, no talk! I'm writing you because I'll be in meetings all day and won't be able to take any calls. I have something urgent that I need your help with.

As you know, Comma Cola has hit a sales slump recently. Our market research has shown that we are no longer popular with 18-30 year olds. Our research has led us to conclude that people in this age range are concerned with their health. They want less fat and sugar in their diet, that's why they don't want to drink Comma Cola. So we've decided to bring out a new brand!

It will be a "healthy" soft-drink. There will be no sugar added, and fruit juice will be used to flavor it. We are pretty sure it will be a success— if the ad campaign is creative enough!

That's where you come in. We hope that your team can come up with a concept for us, as soon as possible. In fact, we'd like you to come to Denver this week, so that we can give you samples of the product and describe it to you in more detail.

Please respond ASAP.
Yours truly,
Mike Waters

To: Mike@commacola.com
Sender: George@creativecodes.com
Subject: Re: Urgent help needed!

Hello Mike,

I will fly out to Denver tomorrow morning. I have reserved a seat on a flight arriving at around two pm, and I will be staying at the Sheraton. My secretary will contact yours with all the details.

Looking forward to this new project,

George Pascal

喬治姨丈的電子郵件

收件者：George@creativecodes.com

寄件者：Mike@commacola.com

主題：緊急求助

哈囉，喬治：

很久沒和你聊聊了。我會寫信給你是因為我整天都要開會，無法接打任何電話。我有件很緊急的事，需要你的幫忙。

你知道，可麥可樂最近遭遇到銷量下跌的情況。我們的市場研究顯示我們的產品，在年齡十八至三十歲之間的人口中，已經不再受歡迎了。我們的研究引導出一個結論：這個年齡層的人關心他們的健康，他們希望飲食中少點脂肪以及糖份。這就是為何他們不想喝可麥可樂的原因。因此我們決定要推出新的品牌。

它將是個「健康」的汽水。無添加糖分，並且會以天然果汁增加風味。我們很確定這個產品會成功，當然更需要廣告商業活動來促成。

這就是要你幫忙的地方了。我們希望你的團隊能夠儘快為我們想出一個廣告概念。事實上，我們希望你這個星期到丹佛來，這樣我們可以提供你產品的樣品，並且向你陳述更多的細節。

請儘快回覆

你真誠的

麥可・瓦特

收件者：Mike@commacola.com

寄件者：George@creativecodes.com

主題：回應：緊急求助

哈囉，麥可！

我明天早上會搭機前往丹佛。我已經訂了機票，大約下午兩點到達，同時住喜來登飯店。我的秘書會跟你的秘書連絡細節部分。

很期待這個新計劃

喬治・巴斯卡

 **Vocabulary**

sender	寄件者
urgent	緊急的
meeting	開會；見面
slump	下滑；下跌
market	市場
research	研究
conclude	結論
range	範圍

concern	關心
diet	節食；飲食控制
brand	品牌
flavor	風味
campaign	商業活動
concept	概念；點子
reserve	保留
secretary	秘書
contact	聯繫；接觸

Useful Sentences

◎ ASAP 盡速

as soon as possible
儘快

A: Can you take this letter to the post office? It needs to go into the mail today!
你可以把信拿去郵局嗎？它今天得寄出去。

B: No problem. I'll leave ASAP!
沒問題，我會儘快拿去。

◎ Look forward to something 期待某事

used to say that one is happy that something will happen in the future
用以說明對某事樂觀其成

A: Are you nervous about meeting my parents at dinner tonight?
今晚要跟我的父母見面，你緊張嗎？

B: Not at all! In fact, I'm looking forward to meeting them!
一點也不！事實上，我很期待跟他們見面。

 **Review Questions**

1. Why is Mike's message "urgent"?

   A) because his company is having a problem with sales

   B) because he no longer enjoys drinking Comma Cola

   C) because it's not very important

   D) because he is too busy to write ASAP

2. Who is not buying Comma Cola these days?

   A) Mike Waters

   B) George Pascal

   C) people between the age of eighteen to thirty

   D) people under the age of eighteen

3. Why might they not be buying Comma Cola?

   A) They think it is not healthy.

   B) They think there is not enough sugar in it.

   C) They don't like its flavor.

   D) They dislike its name.

4. What is used to flavor Comma Cola's new product?

   A) sugar   B) fat

   C) fruit juice   D) water

5. How can George help?

A) by staying at the Sheraton

B) by talking with his secretary

C) by sharing his creative ideas

D) by replying as late as possible

測驗題庫中譯

1. 為什麼麥可的信息很「緊急」？

A) 因為他的公司面臨銷售問題

B) 因為他再也不愛喝可麥可樂了

C) 因為不是很重要

D) 因為他太忙了不能儘快寫信

2. 最近什麼人不購買可麥可樂了？

A) 麥可·瓦特　　　　　　B) 喬治·巴斯卡

C) 十八歲到三十歲的人　　D) 十八歲以下的人

3. 他們不買可麥可樂的可能原因是什麼？

A) 他們認為它不健康　　　B) 他們認為它的含糖量不夠多

C) 他們不喜歡其味道　　　D) 他們不喜歡它的名字

4. 什麼用來增加可麥可樂新產品的風味?

    A) 糖   B) 油脂

    C) 天然果汁   D) 水

5. 喬治要如何幫忙?

    A) 留在喜來登飯店   B) 和他的秘書談談

    C) 提供他的創意點子   D) 儘可能晚一點回應

Unit 4 I'm Going out of Town!

Uncle George gets home at six-thirty. Aunt June greets him at the front door.

Aunt June :   How was your day honey? You must be starving!

Uncle George : Well, I am pretty hungry.

Aunt June :   Did something happen to your lunch again today?

Uncle George : Actually, no, I got to eat my lunch. And thank you, it was delicious!

Aunt June :   I'm glad you were able to enjoy it!

Uncle George : The reason why I'm hungry is because I've had such a busy day today!

Aunt June :   Tell me about it.

Uncle George : At dinner, honey. First I'd like to wash up.

Aunt June :   Sure! Dinner will be ready in twenty minutes.

Uncle George : I'll be there with bells on!

Twenty minutes later, Uncle George joins Aunt June at the dinner table.

Uncle George : My, it's quiet around here! Where are Eric and Lydia?

Aunt June : They've gone out for dinner and a movie with Eric's friends.

Uncle George : I thought Eric was grounded...

Aunt June : Yes, but he's been so good lately. All of his homework has been graded with A's, and I spoke to his teacher today- apparently his attitude is much better.

Uncle George : I'm so happy to hear that!

Aunt June : So, what's your news?

Uncle George : Oh yes! Well, it turns out that I am going to be taking a business trip.

Aunt June : That's exciting! You haven't been out of town for a while.

Uncle George : Yes, most of my clients are here in L.A., but Mike Waters of Comma Cola hopes that I can be of some use out in Denver.

Aunt June : Denver?! That's far away!

Uncle George : It is. That's why I'll be leaving

tomorrow morning.

Aunt June：　　　　So soon?

Uncle George：　Yes, it's urgent business.

我要出城去

喬治姨丈在六點半回到家，茱兒阿姨在前門迎接他。

茱兒阿姨：　親愛的，今天過得怎樣？你一定餓壞了。

喬治姨丈：　是啊，我非常餓。

茱兒阿姨：　今天午餐又出問題了嗎？

喬治姨丈：　事實上沒有。我吃了我的午餐。還要謝謝妳，午餐非常美味。

茱兒阿姨：　我很高興你喜歡。

喬治姨丈：　我餓的原因是因為，我今天實在太忙了。

茱兒阿姨：　說來聽聽吧。

喬治姨丈：　親愛的，晚餐時再說吧。我想先洗澡。

茱兒阿姨：　好！晚餐在二十分鐘內會準備好。

喬治姨丈：　我會愉快地出現的。

二十分鐘後，喬治姨丈加入了飯桌。

喬治姨丈：　老天，這裡好安靜！艾瑞克和麗迪亞呢？

茱兒阿姨：　他們和艾瑞克的朋友出去吃晚餐、看電影了。

喬治姨丈：　我以為艾瑞克是不准出門的……

茱兒阿姨：　是啊，不過他最近很乖。他所有的作業都拿到 A，而且我今天跟他的老師談過，他的上課態度很明顯

地進步許多。

喬治姨丈：我很高興聽到這個。

茱兒阿姨：那麼，你的新聞呢？

喬治姨丈：　喔，對了！是這樣的，我得出城做一趟商務之旅。

茱兒阿姨：　那真令人興奮！你已經有一陣子沒出城了。

喬治姨丈：　是啊，大部分的客戶都在洛杉磯這裡，但是可麥可樂的麥可‧瓦特希望我能到丹佛去幫忙。

茱兒阿姨：　丹佛？那好遠啊。

喬治姨丈：　是啊，這就是為什麼我明天早上就得動身了。

茱兒阿姨：　這麼快？

喬治姨丈：　是啊，這是一筆緊急的生意。

Vocabulary

actually	事實上
honey	親愛的
wash up	清洗；洗乾淨
take a trip	旅行
go out of town	出城；離開居住的地方
be of some use	能夠有所幫助

Useful Sentences

◎ Be there with bells on　十分樂意

used to say that one will be very happy to be in a place or to do something
用以說明某人樂意出席或從事某事

A:　Are you sure you really want to come watch my school play? It may not be very good.
你確定你真的想來看我的校內比賽？也許不會很精采喔。

B:　Don't be silly. Of course I'd love to come. I'll be there with bells on!
別傻了！我當然想去看。我會很樂意到場的。

◎ Apparently　明顯地

so it seems
似乎是這樣

A:　I've heard that it's going to rain tomorrow.
我聽說明天會下雨。

B:　Apparently, so does the weatherman. He told us to expect a typhoon soon!
很可能，氣象播報員也這樣說；他說很快就會有一個颱風來了。

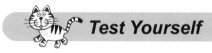 Test Yourself

1. Who greets Uncle George at six thirty?

   A) his employees   B) his wife

   C) his son   D) his niece

2. Why is Uncle George hungry?

   A) Someone stole his lunch.

   B) His lunch was thrown away.

   C) He had a very busy day.

   D) He couldn't eat in Denver.

3. What time do Aunt June and Uncle George sit down at the dinner table?

   A) six thirty   B) six forty

   C) six fifty   D) seven o'clock

4. Where are Eric and Lydia?

   A) out with Eric's friends   B) in Denver

   C) at the dinner table   D) washing up

5. Why is Aunt June surprised that Uncle George is taking a trip?

   A) because his business is having a sales slump

   B) because he had promised to take her on vacation

C) because he is afraid of flying on planes

D) because he hasn't gone out of town for a long time.

 測驗題庫中譯

1. 誰在六點半時迎接喬治姨丈？

    A) 他的員工   B) 他的妻子   C) 他的兒子   D) 他的姪女

2. 喬治姨丈為什麼很餓？

    A) 有人偷了他的午餐   B) 他的午餐被丟掉了

    C) 他一整天都很忙   D) 他無法在丹佛吃東西

3. 茱兒阿姨和喬治姨丈幾點坐在晚餐桌前？

    A) 六點半   B) 六點四十   C) 六點五十   D) 七點

4. 艾瑞克和麗迪亞去哪了？

    A) 和艾瑞克的朋友出去了   B) 在丹佛

    C) 在晚餐桌前   D) 在洗澡

5. 為什麼茱兒阿姨對於喬治姨丈的旅行感到驚訝？

    A) 因為他的生意正面臨銷售下跌   B) 因為他保證過帶她去渡假

    C) 因為他害怕搭飛機   D) 因為他已經很久沒出城了

Unit 5

Preparing for the Trip

It isn't simple to organize a trip, especially one on the spur of the moment. Luckily, Uncle George has a good travel agent. She was able to book him a flight and a hotel room in Denver. Though, since the trip is last minute, he will have to pay a lot more money.

But before he even gets on the plane, there are lots of things that Uncle George has to do first. He has to call a taxi company and arrange for a cab to come and take him to the airport. He must go to the bank and get enough cash to last him through his trip. But most importantly, Uncle George has to pack!

Packing a suitcase is never easy for Uncle George. That's because he always brings too much stuff. He worries that he may need something while he's away, and puts it in his bag just in case. This time, Uncle George needs to bring a couple of suits, a good pair of shoes, underwear, pajamas and toiletries. However, in his suitcase there are about five pairs of shoes, seven suits, four books, three sweaters and a pair of cowboy boots! Luckily for Uncle George, Aunt June is much more practical. When he goes to sleep tonight, she will go through his bag and take out the stuff that he doesn't need to take with him.

為旅程做準備

　　要規劃一趟旅程並不容易，尤其是在緊急的情況下。幸好，喬治姨丈有很好的旅行社，她為他訂機位以及丹佛的旅館房間。不過，由於旅程很晚才確定，他得付更高的價錢。

　　但是在他上飛機前，有許多事情是喬治姨丈必須先做的。他得打電話給計程車行，安排一輛車接送他去機場。他得到銀行去領取足夠的現金以供他旅程使用。但最重要的是，喬治姨丈得裝箱打包。

　　對喬治姨丈而言，整理行李箱從來不是容易的事，因為他總是帶太多行李了。他擔心當他外出時可能會需要某樣東西，為了以防萬一就把它放進袋裡。這一次，喬治姨丈只需要帶兩個箱子、一雙好鞋子、內衣褲、睡衣褲和盥洗用具。然而，他的手提箱裡面卻有五雙鞋子、七套西裝、四本書、三件毛衣和一雙牛仔靴。喬治姨丈很幸運，因為茱兒阿姨比他實際多了。他今晚去睡覺，她就會打開他的行李，把不需要帶的東西都拿出來。

Vocabulary

simple	簡單的;容易的
organize	組織
travel agent	旅行社
book	訂 (機票等)
arrange	安排
cab	計程車
cash	現金
pack	打包
suitcase	手提箱
suit	西裝
underwear	內衣褲
pajamas	寬鬆的睡衣褲
toiletries	盥洗用具;化妝品
practical	實際的

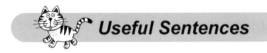 **Useful Sentences**

◎ On the spur of the moment 迫在眉梢

done without planning at the very latest opportunity
到最後關頭才決定去做

A: I didn't know that you were going to come to the party tonight!
我不知道妳今晚要來派對。

B: I decided to come on the spur of the moment.
我是在最後關頭才決定要來的。

◎ Just in case 以防萬一

when something is done in order to make sure that something else will (or will not) happen
做某事是為了確保另一件事將來會（或者不會）發生

A: You should take an umbrella with you when you go out, just in case it rains.
你出門時應該帶把傘，以防下雨。

B: Good idea! Thanks.
好主意！謝啦！

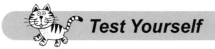

Test Yourself

1. What can we say about Uncle George's trip?

   A) He spent a lot of time planning it.

   B) The decision to take it was sudden.

   C) He does not have enough time to pack for it.

   D) He is unwilling to go.

2. Why will Uncle George have to pay more for his trip?

   A) because it is last minute

   B) because he is going first-class

   C) because he is not a wise businessman

   D) because he is traveling with his wife

3. What does Uncle George not need to do himself?

   A) pack his bags   B) call a cab

   C) get money from the bank   D) book a hotel room

4. Why is Uncle George bad at packing a bag?

   A) He always wants to take too much.

   B) He never wants to use a suitcase.

C) He never takes the things he just might need.

D) He always takes too little.

5. What can we say about Aunt June?

A) She will not help Uncle George.

B) She is jealous that her husband is going on a trip.

C) She is more practical than her husband.

D) She doesn't think he should take any clothes with him.

測驗題庫中譯

1. 我們可以怎麼形容喬治姨丈的旅行？

　　A) 他花了很多時間計畫　　　　B) 旅行的決定十分突然

　　C) 他沒有足夠時間打包　　　　D) 他不願意去

2. 為什麼喬治姨丈這次旅行必須付比較多錢？

　　A) 因為旅程確定得太晚　　　B) 因為他坐頭等艙

　　C) 因為他不是個聰明的生意人　D) 因為他帶著妻子一起旅行

3. 喬治姨丈不需要親自做什麼事情？

　　A) 打包行李　　　　　　　　B) 叫計程車

　　C) 從銀行領錢　　　　　　　D) 訂旅館房間

4. 為什麼喬治姨丈不擅於打包行李？

　　A) 他總是想帶太多東西　　　B) 他從不想使用手提箱

　　C) 他從來不帶可能需要用到的東西　D) 他總是帶太少東西

5. 我們可以怎麼形容茱兒阿姨？

　　A) 她不會幫助喬治姨丈　　　B) 她忌妒她的丈夫要去旅行

　　C) 她比她丈夫實際　　　　　D) 她認為他無須帶任何衣服

Unit 6 At the Airport

Uncle George is in a cab on his way to the airport. The driver speaks to him.

Driver :	Which terminal do you need; international or domestic departures?
Uncle George :	Domestic. I'm just going to Denver.
Driver :	Sure thing. OK! Here we are.
Uncle George :	What does the meter read?
Driver :	Forty-seven eighty.
Uncle George :	Here's fifty. You can keep the change.
Driver :	Do you need a hand with your luggage?
Uncle George :	No, thanks. You can just open the trunk, and I'll be fine. My suitcase is surprisingly light!

Uncle George goes to the check-in counter.

Clerk :	Ticket please.
Uncle George :	Here you go!
Clerk :	Thank you. Would you like an aisle seat, or a window seat?

Uncle George : I'd prefer a window seat, thanks. I
like having a view!

Clerk : Is there anyone traveling with
you today, sir?

Uncle George : No, just me.

Clerk : Do you have any baggage to check?

Uncle George : Just this one.

Clerk : OK, here is you baggage claim
ticket. Enjoy your flight!

Uncle George : Thank you!

Uncle George is waiting in the airport lounge until his flight's departure time is announced. He begins chatting with another passenger.

Uncle George : Say, do you have the time?

Passenger : Yes. It's eleven o'clock.

Uncle George : Really? I'm taking a flight to Denver,
and the boarding time was supposed
to be twenty minutes ago.

Passenger : I'm taking that flight too. A few
minutes ago, they announced that
the flight would be delayed.

Uncle George : No kidding! I wonder what for?

Passenger :   I think there is a small
                mechanical problem. But they
                should have it fixed soon.

在機場

喬治姨丈坐在計程車裡前往機場的路上。計程車司機跟他說話。

司機：　　　你要到哪個航廈？國際航廈還是國內航廈？

喬治姨丈：　國內的。我只是要去丹佛。

司機：　　　沒問題。好，我們到了。

喬治姨丈：　表跳了多少？

司機：　　　四十七元八十分錢。

喬治姨丈：　這裡是五十元。不用找了。

司機：　　　要我幫忙提行李嗎？

喬治姨丈：　不用了，謝謝。你只要打開後車廂就好了，我可以
　　　　　　自己來。我的手提箱比我想像中輕很多呢。

喬治姨丈到了報到櫃檯。

服務員：　　請給我機票。

喬治姨丈：　在這裡。

服務員：　　謝謝。你想要靠走道的座位還是靠窗戶的？

喬治姨丈：　我想要靠窗的位置，謝謝。我喜歡看風景。

服務員：　　先生，今天有人跟你一起旅行嗎？

喬治姨丈： 沒有，只有我自己。

服務員： 有任何行李箱要託運嗎？

喬治姨丈： 只有這一個。

服務員： 好的，這是你的行李箱提領單。祝你旅途愉快。

喬治姨丈： 謝謝。

喬治姨丈在機場大廳等著，直到廣播他的班機駛離時間。
他開始跟另外一個乘客交談。

喬治姨丈： 嘿，你知道幾點了嗎？

乘客： 十一點了。

喬治姨丈： 真的嗎？我要搭到丹佛的班機，登機時間不是應該
在二十分鐘以前嗎？

乘客： 我也搭那班班機。幾分鐘以前有廣播説，這個班機
會誤點。

喬治姨丈： 不會吧！為什麼？

乘客： 我想是因為一點機器上的小問題。但是他們應該很
快就會修好。

 **Vocabulary**

terminal	終點站；航廈
international	國際的
domestic	國內的

departure	離開
meter	表；計；公尺
luggage	行李
trunk	後車廂
surprisingly	令人驚訝地
light	輕盈的
check-in	報到；登記
counter	櫃檯
baggage	行李
window	窗戶
aisle	走道
passenger	乘客
announce	廣播；宣布
delay	延誤
mechanical	機器的

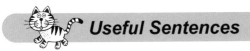 **Useful Sentences**

◎ A hand 援手

help
幫忙

A: Can I give you a hand with those bags? They look awfully heavy!
我幫你提那些行李好嗎？它們看起來很重。

B: Thank you! They are very heavy, so be careful!
謝謝。它們真的很重，要小心一點。

◎ No kidding 不會吧

used to express surprise or disbelief
用以表達驚訝或者不相信

A: My grandmother will be 100 years old next month.
我奶奶下個月要滿一百歲了。

B: No kidding!
不會吧！

 **Test Yourself**

1. How does Uncle George get to the LA airport?

    A) He flies.   B) He drives his car.

    C) Aunt June drives him.   D) He takes a cab.

2. Which terminal does Uncle George need to go to?

    A) international arrivals   B) international departures

    C) domestic arrivals   D) domestic departures

3. How many pieces of luggage does Uncle George
check in?

    A) one   B) two

    C) three   D) four

4. Why does Uncle George want a window seat?

    A) He thinks it's safer.

    B) There is more space by the window.

    C) He'd like to see the view.

    D) It's closer to the bathroom.

5. Why is the plane delayed?

A) Not all the passengers have arrived yet.

B) The weather is stopping it from leaving.

C) The pilots have not shown up yet.

D) There is a mechanical problem.

 測驗題庫中譯

1. 喬治姨丈怎麼到洛杉磯機場？

A) 搭飛機   B) 他開車

C) 茱兒阿姨開車載他   D) 搭計程車

2. 喬治姨丈要到哪個航廈？

A) 國際入境   B) 國際離境   C) 國內抵達   D) 國內駛離

3. 喬治姨丈有幾件行李要登記？

A) 一件   B) 二件   C) 三件   D) 四件

4. 為什麼喬治姨丈想要靠窗的位置？

A) 他認為這樣安全些   B) 靠窗的空間較大

C) 他喜歡看風景   D) 比較接近洗手間

5. 為什麼班機延誤了？

A) 有乘客尚未到達   B) 天氣狀況使得班機無法離開

C) 駕駛員尚未出現   D) 出現了一點機器上的問題

Chapter ④ Aunt June

茱兒阿姨

Unit 1 Aunt June

Aunt June is a busy woman. Not only does she teach art part-time at the local elementary school, but she is also an artist. She has a studio downtown, and she spends about twenty hours a week there working on her paintings. Her latest project is a series of landscapes of the city's different neighborhoods.

Ever since June was a little girl, she had enjoyed painting and drawing. When she was in high school, one of her teachers noticed her talent and tutored her privately after school. With his help, June had the confidence to apply for and win a scholarship to art school in France!

June returned to L.A. after three years in Paris. She looked for a job, but it wasn't easy to find one. She tried to get a position in a museum or an art gallery, but nothing was available. So she decided to go back to school and get a degree in teaching. She thought it would be a good idea to make a living teaching others how to do what she loved to do most herself.

The good thing about teaching is that June gets the summers off. This was a good thing for her when Eric was a little boy. It meant that she could stay home with him when he wasn't in school. But now that he is old enough to look after himself, having the summers off means that June can spend more time on her art. June feels very lucky to have this time right now because next month, she is showing her work in a downtown gallery. She has a lot to do to prepare for it.

Today, however, Aunt June isn't going to be spending much time in the studio. She has some errands to do-and she also wants to take Lydia out. She feels badly that she hasn't had much time to spend with her niece. Ages ago, she promised to take Lydia shopping - so she'll be killing two birds with one stone!

茱兒阿姨

茱兒阿姨是個忙碌的女性。不只因為她在當地小學兼職教美術，同時也因為她是個藝術家。她在市區有個工作室，而且一個禮拜會花大概二十個小時在那裡畫畫。她最新的計劃是一系列城裡不同區的風景畫。

　　當茱兒還是一個小女孩時，她就一直很喜歡畫畫和塗鴉。念高中的時候，她的一位老師注意到她的天份，並且在放學後私底下教導她。在他的幫助下，茱兒有了信心並申請到了法國藝術學校的獎學金。

　　在巴黎待了三年後，茱兒回到洛杉磯。她找工作並不順利。她想找博物館或者畫廊的職務，但卻一無所獲。於是她決定回學校，修取教師學位。她認為，可以拿自己的專長與興趣來教導別人，應該是不錯的出路。

　　茱兒教書的好處是，她可以放暑假。當艾瑞克還是個小男孩時，這點對她而言是很有利的。這意謂著當小艾瑞克不用上學時，她可以留在家裡陪他。但是現在他已經夠大可以照顧自己了，放暑假意謂著她能夠花更多時間在她的藝術上。茱兒覺得現在能擁有這些時間相當幸運，因為下個月她就要在市區裡的美術館展出她的作品了。她得為它做好多準備。

　　然而，今天茱兒阿姨不會花那麼多時間待在工作室裡。她有一些瑣事要做──而且她也想帶麗迪亞出去走走。對於沒有太多時間陪伴她的姪女，她覺得很抱歉。老早以前，她就答應過麗迪亞要帶她去逛街購物──這樣一來她就可以一舉兩得了。

Vocabulary

part-time	兼職
elementary school	小學

studio	工作室
work on something	從事某事；做某事
latest	最近的；最新的
landscape	景觀
tutor	當家庭教師
privately	私下地；私人地
confidence	信心
apply for	申請
scholarship	獎學金
gallery	畫廊
museum	博物館
make a living	維生
degree	學位；等級
errand	差事；使命，任務

Useful Sentences

◎ Not only... but also... 不但……也……

used to give more information about something
用以給予某事更多的訊息

A: Your dad is a great cook! The hamburgers he made us for dinner last night were delicious!
你爸爸的廚藝真是太好了。他昨天晚餐為我們做的漢堡非常好吃。

B: Not only can my dad make great hamburgers, but he can also make good pizza!
我爸爸不僅能夠做出好吃的漢堡，他還會做好吃的披薩。

◎ A series of 一系列

a group of things related to one another, usually happening in a sequence relating to time or space
通常是指發生在同樣的時間或空間上相關連的事

A: What happened at the police station?
在警察局發生什麼事情了？

B: I was asked a series of questions about what I saw the night of the robbery, and then they let me leave.
他們問我一連串昨晚目擊的搶劫事件，然後他們就讓我走了。

◎ Time off **放假**

a period of time when one does not have to work, go to school, or do anything that one would normally need to do
無須工作、上學，或者不用做例行事物的一段時間

A: Will you be going to America again this year for winter vacation?
今年寒假你還要再去美國嗎？

B: No, I'm afraid that I couldn't get any time off from my job.
不了，我的工作恐怕無法休假。

◎ Kill two birds with one stone **一舉兩得**

to accomplish two things with one action
採取一個行動就達到兩個目的

A: On your way to take the garbage out, can you check our mailbox to see if there's anything inside?
去丟垃圾時，你可以順便看一下我們的信箱有沒有郵件嗎？

B: Sure, that way I'll be killing two birds with one stone.
沒問題，這是一舉兩得的好主意。

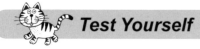 **Test Yourself**

1. Which of the following has Aunt June never done?

   A) work with children   B) lead tours in a museum

   C) study abroad   D) paint pictures

2. Where is Aunt June's studio?

   A) in her classroom   B) in her neighborhood

   C) in France   D) downtown

3. What did June's high school art teacher notice ?

   A) her natural ability   B) her poor habits

   C) her excellent French   D) her skill with children

4. What did not happen after June returned from Paris?

   A) She went back to school.

   B) She gave up on art.

   C) She tried to find a job.

   D) She decided to make a living doing what she loved.

5. What is a benefit to June's job as a teacher?

   A) She must work at the school all the time.

   B) She can take her son to school with her.

C) She can have time off to do other things.

D) She can teach; which is what she loves to do most.

6. What can we say about June?

    A) She cares about her son and about her career as an artist.

    B) She only cares about her career as a teacher.

    C) She only cares about her art.

    D) She only cares about her son.

7. Why is June busy these days?

    A) She is getting ready to show her work in a gallery.

    B) She has too many students in her class.

    C) Lydia is taking up too much of her time.

    D) Her son needs a lot of attention now that he's older.

8. What will June do today?

    A) go to art school   B) work in her studio

    C) spend time with Lydia   D) raise her son

9. What will Lydia do today?

    A) stay at home alone

    B) kill birds using a stone

C) go shopping with her aunt

D) learn about painting

10. How did Aunt June feel about not spending time with Lydia?

A) fine

B) badly

C) sick

D) angry

 測驗題庫中譯

1. 下列何者是茱兒阿姨從沒做過的？

　A) 和孩子一起工作　　　　　　B) 在博物館中導覽

　C) 出國唸書　　　　　　　　　D) 畫圖

2. 茱兒阿姨的工作室在哪裡？

　A) 在她的教室裡　　　　　　　B) 在她家附近

　C) 在法國　　　　　　　　　　D) 在市區

3. 茱兒的高中老師注意到什麼事情？

　A) 她的天份　　　　　　　　　B) 她的壞習慣

　C) 她流利的法語　　　　　　　D) 她對待孩子的技巧

4. 茱兒從巴黎回來後，什麼事情沒有發生過？

　A) 她回到學校唸書　　　　　　B) 她放棄藝術

C) 她試圖找工作　D) 她決定以她所愛的事物作為維生的工具

5. 茉兒當老師的工作有什麼好處？

A) 她必須一天到晚在學校工作　　B) 她可以帶著她兒子到學校

C) 她可以有休假時間做其他事情　D) 她可以教學，這是她最愛的事情

6. 我們可以怎麼形容茉兒？

A) 她在乎她的兒子以及她作為一個藝術家的生涯

B) 她只在乎她的教師生涯　　C) 她只關心她的藝術

D) 她只關心她的兒子

7. 為什麼茉兒最近很忙？

A) 她準備在畫廊展出她的作品　B) 她班上有太多學生

C) 麗迪亞佔據她太多時間　　　D) 她的兒子長大了，需要更多關愛

8. 今天茉兒要做什麼？

A) 去藝術學校　　　　　　　B) 在工作室工作

C) 花時間陪麗迪亞　　　　　D) 養育她的兒子

9. 麗迪亞今天要做什麼？

A) 獨自留在家裡面　　　　　B) 用石頭打死鳥兒

C) 跟她阿姨去逛街購物　　　D) 學習怎麼畫圖

10. 茉兒沒有花時間陪麗迪亞，她有什麼感覺？

A) 無所謂　　B) 很糟糕　　C) 不舒服　　D) 生氣

 Take a Peek

Aunt June asks Lydia if she's ready to go out.

Lydia :   I am! So, what are we going to do today, anyway?

Aunt June :   Well, I have a few errands that I have to run. But after that it's up to you.

Lydia :   I've got carte blanche?

Aunt June :   Pretty much. As long as we can drive there, we can do it.

Lydia :   That's great, but there's a problem. I haven't a clue where to go.

Aunt June :   Well, why don't you take a peek at this L.A. guidebook? You can read up on the shopping districts and some of the local attractions.

Lydia :   Good idea.

Aunt June :   You can check out the newspaper for restaurant listings. I'm taking you out for lunch, and you can choose where we eat. So, are you ready to go?

Lydia :   Well, I'm not so sure anymore. It

looks like I've got a lot of reading to do!

Aunt June : You can look through the paper and guidebook in the car while I'm doing my errands. It should give you about an hour to decide!

Lydia : All right then! Let's hit the road!

閱覽

茱兒阿姨問麗迪亞她是否準備好要出門了。

麗迪亞： 我好了！那麼，我們今天到底要做什麼呢？

茱兒阿姨： 這個嘛，我得跑一些差事，但在那之後就由你決定囉。

麗迪亞： 我可以全權做主嗎？

茱兒阿姨： 完全沒錯。只要我們開車可以到達，什麼事情都可以。

麗迪亞： 太好了，但是有一個問題。我不知道要到哪裡去。

茱兒阿姨： 那麼，你為什麼不看一下洛杉磯的導覽手冊呢？你可以看一下購物區以及一些當地的景點。

麗迪亞： 好主意！

茱兒阿姨： 你也可以看一下報紙的餐廳介紹。我帶你去吃午餐，你可以選擇我們用餐的地點。那麼，你準備好要出發了嗎？

麗迪亞： 這樣啊，我不確定耶。看來我要看好多東西哦。

茱兒阿姨： 你可以利用我去辦事的時候，在車上看報紙和導覽手冊。你應該有一個小時可以做決定。

麗迪亞： 那好！那我們上路吧！

Vocabulary

peek	窺視
guidebook	導覽手冊；旅行指南
district	地區；區域
attractions	景點
listing	列表；名單
take somebody out	帶某人外出

 *Useful Sentences*

◎ It's up to you 由你決定

somebody else's decision to make
由別人做決定

A: Do you want to eat at an Indian restaurant tonight, or at a Chinese one?
你今晚想要在印度餐廳或者中國餐廳吃飯呢？

B: Either one is fine for me. It's up to you!
兩個我都可以。你決定吧！

◎ To have carte blanche 全權作主

to have the freedom to do whatever one wants
可以做任何自己想做的事

A: So do I have carte blanche to decorate my room?
我可以依自己的意思佈置房間嗎？

B: I'm afraid not. Your walls must be white, and you can't hang any posters on them.
恐怕不行。你的牆壁必須是白色的，而且你也不能掛任何海報在上面。

◎ I don't have a clue **我不知道**

to have no idea about something
對於某事一無所知

A: Can you guess what's in this box?
你可以猜猜盒子裡面有什麼嗎？

B: I don't have a clue! Tell me, then.
我完全不知道。告訴我吧。

◎ Hit the road **上路**

to leave a place and go somewhere else
離開一個地方到另一個地方去

A: I'm tired of this party. No one seems to be having any fun at all.
我對這個派對厭煩透頂。似乎沒半個人覺得好玩。

B: We don't have to stay. Let me say goodbye to the hosts, and then we can hit the road.
我們不必留下來。我去跟主人說再見，然後我們就離開吧。

 **Test Yourself**

1. Where does Aunt June suggest Lydia look for ideas on how to spend their afternoon together?

   A) in a guidebook   B) in the bathroom

   C) in the car   D) in a restaurant

2. When will Lydia have time to decide on where to go?

   A) at the restaurant

   B) while Aunt June does her errands

   C) before they leave the house

   D) after an afternoon in L.A.

3. What can Lydia find in the newspaper?

   A) Aunt June's errands   B) a place to eat lunch

   C) the time a movie will begin

   D) the location of a good barber

4. How long will it take Aunt June to do her errands?

   A) about an hour   B) two hours

   C) almost three hours   D) over four hours

5. Where will Lydia be while June is doing her errands?

    A) at a restaurant   B) at home

    C) in a park   D) in the car

測驗題庫中譯

1. 茱兒阿姨建議麗迪亞到哪裡尋找，下午該去哪兒的意見呢？

    A) 導覽手冊   B) 洗手間   C) 車子上   D) 在餐廳裡面

2. 麗迪亞何時有空檔決定要去哪呢？

    A) 在餐廳時   B) 當茱兒阿姨去辦事情時

    C) 在她們離開家前   D) 在洛杉磯的一個午後

3. 麗迪亞可以在報紙裡面找到什麼？

    A) 茱兒阿姨的差事   B) 吃午餐的地方

    C) 電影開演時間   D) 一家好理髮廳的地點

4. 茱兒阿姨的差事要辦多久呢？

    A) 大約一個小時   B) 兩小時

    C) 幾乎三個小時   D) 超過四個小時

5. 當茱兒阿姨在辦事情時，麗迪亞會在哪裡？

    A) 在餐廳裡   B) 在家裡面

    C) 在公園裡面   D) 在車子裡

Unit 3 The Travel Smart Guide to L.A.

While Aunt June is driving, Lydia opens up her guidebook, The Travel Smart Guide to L.A. It's a big book, and Lydia opens it to the first chapter which is an introduction to the city.

The Travel Smart Guide to L.A.

Welcome to Los Angeles, the City of Angels! Many visitors who come here are amazed, and sometimes confused, by the large size of this city. It helps to bear in mind that what is normally covered by the blanket term "L.A." is in fact a group of 88 separate cities!

Visitors most commonly spend time west of downtown L.A. This is the home of Hollywood, and, a little further west, dozens of celebrities. In the neighborhoods of Beverly Hills, Bel Air, and Brentwood, live some of the country's richest and most famous people!

Forming the northern border of L.A. county is the San Fernando Valley. Though not particularly beautiful, the San Fernando Valley is of interest to many of L.A.'s visitors as this is the location of many major movie studios. On a trip to L.A. you may not actually see many angels, but we can almost guarantee you'll see a star or two!

About L.A.

Population	L.A. City : 4 million
	L.A. County : 10 million
People	Latino : 45 percent
	Caucasian : 32 percent
	Black : 10 percent
	Asian : 13 percent
Area	L.A. City : 1,200 square kilometers
	L.A. County : 10,600 square kilometers
Climate	Hot dry summers and moderate, wet winters.
Sate	California
Time zone	Pacific Time (GMT -8)

洛杉磯的聰明旅遊指南

　茱兒阿姨開車時，麗迪亞打開了她的導覽手冊：「洛杉磯的聰明旅遊指南」。那是一本很大的書，麗迪亞翻到了第一章，內容是這座城市的介紹。

洛杉磯的聰明旅遊指南

　　歡迎來到天使之城洛杉磯！許多遊客都因這座城市的巨大而感到驚訝，有時還會困惑不解。記住這個事實會很有幫助：洛杉磯這個概括的詞，事實上是由八十八個獨立的城市組合而成。

　　遊客們最常把時間花在洛杉磯市的西區。這裡是好萊塢的發源地，而再西邊一點，則有許多名人。在比佛利山莊、貝爾艾爾以及布蘭特伍德區，住著了一些這個國家裡最有錢、最有名聲的人。

　　作為洛杉磯郡北方屏障的是聖佛蘭多山谷。雖然它不是特別美麗，但聖佛蘭多山谷卻吸引了許多遊客，因為這裡是許多大型主流電影製片廠的所在地。到洛杉磯旅行時，你也許不會真的看到天使，但我們保證你一定會看到一、二個明星！

《 關於洛杉磯 》

人口	洛杉磯市：四百萬人
	洛杉磯郡：一千萬人
種族	拉丁人：百分之四十五
	白種人：百分之三十二
	黑人：百分之十
	亞洲人：百分之十三
面積	洛杉磯市：一千兩百平方公里
	洛杉磯郡：一萬零六百平方公里
氣候	夏天炎熱且乾燥，冬天潮濕且宜人
州屬	加利佛尼亞州
時區	太平洋時區（格林威治時區 -8）

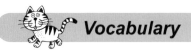 **Vocabulary**

chapter	章節
introduction	介紹
amaze	使驚訝
confuse	使困惑
blanket term	概括的詞彙
separate	個別的；分開的
commonly	普遍地
celebrity	名人
particularly	特別是；特別地
guarantee	保證
population	人口
Latino	拉丁美洲人種
area	面積；地區
square kilometers	平方公里

climate	氣候
time zone	時區

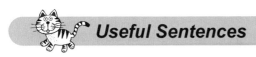 **Useful Sentences**

◎ Bear in mind **謹記**

to remember some aspects of something which may affect one's thinking about it
記住會影響思考方向的關鍵點

A: OK, I'm going to give you your birthday present now. It's nothing expensive, but bear in mind that I'm just a student and I don't have a lot of money.
好，現在我要送你生日禮物了。不是什麼貴重的東西，但是記住，我只是個學生，我沒有什麼錢。

B: Don't worry so much! It's the thought that counts!
別擔心。重要的是心意。

◎ Be home to　家鄉

to be the place where somebody or something resides
某人或某事所屬的地方

A: Why are you going to New York for your vacation? Why not go to a warm beach somewhere?
為什麼你要到紐約渡假呢？為什麼不去溫暖的海灘之類的地方？

B: I'm going because New York is home to the Yankees, my favorite baseball team. While I'm there, I intend to see a couple of games.
我到紐約是因為，那裡是我最愛的棒球隊洋基隊的家鄉。等我到那裡時，我打算去看幾場球賽。

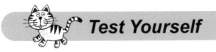 **Test Yourself**

1. Who is the *"The Travel Smart Guide to L.A. "* intended for?

   A) people visiting L.A.

   B) people living in L.A.

   C) people who were born in L.A.

   D) people who write in L.A.

2. What is another name for Los Angeles?

   A) Hollywood   B) The City of Angels

   C) The City of Stars   D) San Fernando

3. How many cities are there in L.A. County?

   A) one   B) eighteen

   C) eighty   D) eighty-eight

4. Where do some of America's richest people live?

   A) in the San Fernando Valley

   B) in Bel Air

   C) in downtown L.A.

   D) in Hollywood

5. Which of the following statements about the San
   Fernando Valley is not true?

   A) It is north of the City of Angels.

   B) Many movies are filmed there.

   C) Visitors find it an interesting place to see.

   D) It has beautiful scenery.

6. What does The Travel Smart Guide to L.A.
   guarantee?

   A) that visitors will feel cold in the summer

   B) that visitors will see celebrities in L.A.

   C) that visitors will meet some angels

   D) that visitors will star in a movie

7. How many people live in L.A. County?

   A) 100,000   B) 1,000,000

   C) 10,000,000   D) 100,000,000

8. How many Asians live in L.A. County?

   A) 13   B) 87,000

   C) 870,000   D) 1,300,000

9. What can we say about winters in L.A.?

   A) They are generally warm and sunny.

   B) They are generally cold and dry.

   C) They are generally mild and rainy.

   D) They are generally hot and wet.

10. Which of the following information is not in the introduction to The Travel Smart Guide to L.A.?

    A) information about the city's history

    B) information about the size of the city

    C) information about the people who live in the city

    D) information about the city's location

 測驗題庫中譯

1. 「洛杉磯聰明旅遊指南」是為誰而作的？

   A) 到洛杉磯玩的人　　　　　B) 住在洛杉磯的人

   C) 出生在洛杉磯的人　　　　D) 在洛杉磯寫作的人

2. 洛杉磯的另一個名字是什麼？

   A) 好萊塢　　B) 天使之城　　C) 明星之城　　D) 聖佛蘭多

3. 洛杉磯郡有多少個城市？

　　A) 一個　　　　　B) 十八個　　　C) 八十個　　　D) 八十八個

4. 美國其中一些最有錢的人住在哪裡？

　　A) 在聖佛蘭多山谷　　　　　B) 在貝爾艾爾

　　C) 在洛杉磯市區　　　　　　D) 在好萊塢

5. 以下哪個關於聖佛蘭多山谷的敘述是錯誤的？

　　A) 她在天使之城的北方　　　　B) 許多電影在哪裡拍攝

　　C) 遊客認為那裡是個很有趣的地方　D) 她擁有美麗的景緻

6.「洛杉磯聰明旅遊指南」保證什麼事情？

　　A) 遊客們在夏天會覺得很冷　　B) 遊客們會在洛杉磯看到名人

　　C) 遊客們會遇見天使　　　　　D) 遊客們會在電影當中演出

7. 多少人住在洛杉磯郡？

　　A) 十萬人　　B) 一百萬人　　　C) 一千萬人　　D) 一億人

8. 有多少亞洲人住在洛杉磯郡？

　　A) 十三個人　B) 八萬七千個人　C) 八十七萬人　D) 一百三十萬人

9. 我們可以怎麼形容洛杉磯的冬天呢？

　　A) 通常溫暖且而陽光普照　　B) 通常又冷又乾

　　C) 通常溫和而多雨　　　　　D) 通常炎熱潮且濕潤

10. 下列何者沒有出現在「洛杉磯聰明旅遊指南」的介紹裡面？

　　A) 有關城市歷史的資訊　　　B) 有關城市大小的資訊

　　C) 有關住在城市居民的種族的資訊　D) 有關城市位置的資訊

Unit 4 Getting Guidance from the Guide

Lydia realizes that she can't read the book cover to cover, so she looks in the book's index to find information about local attractions and shopping. She is amazed by how many listings for shopping she sees and guesses that people from L.A. really like to spend money! She turns to the travel guide's section on shopping, and this is what she reads:

Shopping in L.A.

It's true what you've heard: L.A. loves to shop! From Beverly hills, to Hollywood, L.A. shows its style in countless boutiques, malls, and markets!

Perhaps the most famous shopping district is Rodeo Drive. Located in just a stone's throw from the luxury houses of Beverly Hills, Rodeo Drive is the place to go if you want to find items from famous international designers like Louis Vuitton, Giorgio Armani, or Versace; it's also a great place to go to see the people who shop there! Celebrities flock to Rodeo Drive for the latest fashions, so, for people-watching, and for shopping, this street can't be beat!

Not everyone in L.A. is rich and famous, though most people dress as though they were. Their secret? L.A.'s outlet malls. Located in L.A. County off the city's many freeways are large stores offering last season's designer clothes at big discounts. If it's a combination of style and affordability you're after, this is the place to go.

For travelers on a tight budget, we recommend checking out L.A.'s Hispanic shopping district. Here, in between cheap restaurants and pop-music vendors, you'll find dozens of shops selling great souvenirs of your trip to L.A. The Hispanic shopping district is located just south of the Civic Center.

從導覽中得到指示

　　麗迪亞了解到她無法一頁一頁看這本書,所以她看了書中的索引,尋找有關當地景點以及購物的資訊。她非常訝異書中有那麼多的購物區名單,也猜想或許是洛杉磯人很愛花錢。她翻到旅遊指南的購物篇,以下是她所看到的:

在洛杉磯購物

你所聽說的是真的：洛杉磯人熱愛購物！從比佛利山莊到好萊塢，洛杉磯內數不清的精品店、購物中心和市場都展現出其風格。

最有名的購物區應該是羅迪歐大街，它位於距離比佛利山莊的豪華住宅不遠之處。如果你想要找國際知名的設計師，如路易士·威登、亞曼尼、或是凡塞斯的設計品，羅迪歐大街就是你要去的地方；那也是個觀賞購物人士的好地方。人們為了最新的時尚聚集到羅迪歐大街，因此，對於觀看人群者以及購物者而言，這條街是最好不過了。

並不是每個住在洛杉磯的人都很富有或者有名氣，但大部分人的穿著打扮都煞有其事。他們的秘訣是什麼？是洛杉磯的大型暢貨中心。它位於洛杉磯郡，城市外的許多高速公路邊，矗立許多大型商店，它們提供上一季的設計師服飾，並給予極大的折扣。結合了你所追求的風格以及可負擔價格，是你最好的選擇。

對於預算不多的觀光客而言，我們建議去洛杉磯的希斯佩尼克購物區看看。在這裡，在便宜餐廳以及流行音樂小販之間，你可以找到一大堆洛杉磯旅遊紀念品的商店。希斯佩尼克購物區就位在市民中心的南邊。

Vocabulary

index	索引
attraction	景點
amaze	使驚訝
listing	名單；列表
section	段落；部分
boutique	精品店；流行女裝店
countless	數不清的；無數的
luxury	奢華；昂貴
designer	設計師
outlet	暢貨中心；出口
freeway	高速公路
discount	折扣
vendor	賣主；小販
souvenir	紀念品

Useful Sentences

◎ Read something from cover to cover 仔細地讀

to read everything in a book, magazine, newspaper, etc.
閱讀一本書、雜誌、報紙等的每個部分

A: I'd like to read the newspaper if you're finished with it.
如果你看完報紙了，我想要看。

B: Go ahead. I've read it from cover to cover.
拿去吧。我已經從頭到尾都看過了。

◎ A stone's throw away from 不遠

to be close to or not very far away from a place
距離一個地方非常近或者不太遠

A: Samantha told me you live near Da An Park.
莎曼姍說你住在大安公園附近。

B: She's right. I'm just a stone's throw away!
沒錯。我距離那裡很近。

◎ Flock 聚集

a large group or a particular kind of person who all go to the same location
指同類的群聚動作

A: The library is pretty busy these days.
圖書館最近相當繁忙。

B: That's right. Just before final exams, all the students flock here to study!
沒錯。期末考快到了，所有學生都聚到這裡讀書了。

◎ Can't be beat 再好不過了

to be the best for a particular reason
對於某個特別的原因而言是最好的

A: Your mom's cherry pie can't be beat!
你媽媽的櫻桃派真是完美無缺。

B: I'll tell her you think so-she'll be so happy to hear you like it so much!
我會轉達她的，她會很高興知道你這麼喜歡。

Test Yourself

1. Where is Rodeo Drive?

   A) not far from the homes of many celebrities

   B) in the Hispanic shopping district

   C) a stone's throw from Disneyland

   D) near the freeway

2. What kind of stores can be found on Rodeo Drive?

   A) outlet stores   B) designer stores

   C) cheap music vendors   D) souvenir shops

3. Who normally shops on Rodeo Drive?

   A) tourists on a budget   B) highly paid celebrities

   C) local Hispanics

   D) people looking for discounts

4. If one can't afford to shop on Rodeo Drive, but still wants to look good, where should one go?

   A) the Giorgio Armani shop   B) the Versace boutique

   C) the Hispanic market

   D) the city's designer outlcts

5. Which of the following statements is false?

A) The Hispanic shopping district is south of the Civic Center.

B) Designer outlets offering big discounts are on Rodeo Drive.

C) People who can afford to spend a lot of money shop on Rodeo Drive.

D) The Hispanic shopping district is a great place to pick up things to remind you of your trip to L.A.

 測驗題庫中譯

1. 羅迪歐大街在哪裡？

A) 距離許多名人的住宅不遠處　　B) 在希斯佩尼克購物區

C) 狄斯奈樂園不遠處　　D) 高速公路附近

2. 在羅迪歐大街上可以找到什麼種類的店？

A) 折扣商店　B) 設計師商店　C) 便宜的音樂攤販　D) 紀念品店

3. 哪些人經常在羅迪歐大街購物？

A) 有預算的觀光客　　B) 高價位的名人

C) 當地的希斯佩尼克人　　D) 尋找折扣的人

4. 如果負擔不起羅迪歐大街的消費，但仍想要看起來很氣派，應該去哪裡呢？

A) 亞曼尼商店　　B) 凡塞斯女裝精品店

C) 希斯佩尼克市場　　D) 當地城市的設計師暢貨中心

5. 下列敘述何者是錯誤的？

A) 希斯佩尼克購物區位於市民中心的南邊

B) 提供優惠折扣的設計師商店，位於羅迪歐大街上

C) 可以負擔高價位的人，在羅迪歐大街上購物

D) 希斯佩尼克購物區是個很棒的地方，你可以買到一些有洛杉磯特色的物品

Unit 5 Five Star Reviews

After reading about all of the places to shop in L.A., Lydia decides to check out what The Travel Smart Guide to L.A. has to say about the city's food. In fact, the guide has a lot to say about the city's food. It has an extensive list of restaurant reviews. Here are a few of the ones that Lydia looked at :

Restaurant Reviews

Antoine's Italian Café

This low-key restaurant offers classic Italian dishes and a cozy atmosphere. Head chef, Marco Bellucci, favors simplicity and freshness over trendy dishes. Pizzas, for example, are baked in a traditional wood-burning oven, and sauces are all made from scratch.

The restaurant offers a fine wine list, and a breezy outdoor patio which is perfect for people-watching. Reservations are recommended as Antoine's is a popular place on weekends.

```
Atmosphere:  ★ ★ ★ ★ ☆
Food:        ★ ★ ★ ★ ☆
```

```
┌─────────────────────────────────────┐
│ Service:      ★★★☆☆               │
│ Cost:         $$$                    │
└─────────────────────────────────────┘
```

Zim Zim's

Zim Zim's offers a blend of flavors from East and West. Head chef, David Chen, invites diners to sample Pacific Salmon with Thai curry, and local vegetables spiced up Szechuan-style.

There are many winners on Chen's menu, and Zim Zim's has earned its reputation as the place to go in L.A. to try something new and different. However, though the food is great, Zim Zim's lacks an atmosphere to match. The popular restaurant is over-crowded: it is difficult to have a conversation without raising one's voice, and difficult to cut one's food without bumping elbows with the diners at the next table!

```
┌─────────────────────────────────────┐
│ Atmosphere: ★★☆☆☆                 │
│ Food:        ★★★★★               │
│ Service:     ★★☆☆☆                 │
│ Cost:        $$$$                    │
└─────────────────────────────────────┘
```

The Salad Bar

L.A. is known for being a place where people care about their looks. Thus, you'll find many restaurants here which are devoted to selling health foods. The Salad Bar is one of the best.

As the name implies, there are many salads on offer at The Salad bar, all of them tasty. There is also a great selection of sandwiches and fresh juices, all made to order. Dine-in or take-out.

Atmosphere: ★★★☆☆
Food: ★★★★☆
Service: ★★★☆☆
Cost: $$

Casa Nova

Casa Nova was one of the trendiest restaurants in the city a few years ago. It no longer is, and for good reason: the restaurant's owner, George Brinkman, let success go to his head. Initially the restaurant's appeal came from good food served by interesting people: one's waiter might be a former TV star, or somebody who has been in the news. Part of the fun of a night at Casa Nova's was the chance to chat with one's waiter while enjoying the chef's creations.

Brinkman's big mistake, however, was to lose track of what was happening in the kitchen while focusing on drawing increasingly strange waiters. Now, the food served at Casa Nova tastes like it came out of a tin can, while the employees seem to have been lured from a circus.

Atmosphere:	★ ☆ ☆ ☆ ☆
Food:	☆ ☆ ☆ ☆ ☆
Service:	★ ☆ ☆ ☆ ☆
Cost:	$$$$

五星級評介

在看過了洛杉磯的購物地點之後，麗迪亞決定看看「洛杉磯聰明旅遊指南」對於這個城市的食物作何評論。事實上，導覽裡面有許多關於這個城市的美食介紹，有一長串的餐廳評介。這裡是麗迪亞所看到的其中幾家：

餐廳評介

安東尼義大利餐館

這家低調餐廳供應傳統的義大利餐點以及舒適的氣氛。主廚馬可・貝魯奇偏好簡樸而新鮮的佳餚勝過時下流行的菜色。舉披薩這個例子來說,披薩是用傳統的燃燒木頭的火爐烘烤的,醬料也都是親自以手工製成的。

這家餐廳提供品質優良的紅酒,並且有位於室外、微風徐徐的天井,對於喜歡觀望人潮的顧客是個最完美的地方。安東尼餐館在週末的生意相當好,最好先訂位。

```
氣氛:佳
食物:可口
服務:不錯
價格:中等
```

齊齊泰式料理

齊齊泰式料理呈現的是東西方混合的風味。主廚大衛・陳邀請用餐者體驗以泰國咖哩為沾醬的太平洋鮭魚,搭配四川風味的當地蔬菜。

陳的菜單上有許多獲獎菜餚,而「齊齊」也獲得其名聲,它成為在洛杉磯可以嘗鮮的地點。然而,雖然其食物很棒,「齊齊」卻缺乏可以相搭配的氣氛:這家廣受歡迎的餐廳太過擁擠,如果不提高音量很難跟別人交談,而在切取食物時,手肘也很容易撞到鄰座的

客人。

```
┌ ─ ─ ─ ─ ─ ─ ┐
│ 氣氛：還好      │
│ 食物：很可口    │
│ 服務：還好      │
│ 價格：略高      │
└ ─ ─ ─ ─ ─ ─ ┘
```

沙拉吧

　　洛杉磯是個因愛美而聞名的地方。所以，你會發現這裡的許多餐廳致力於銷售健康食品。「沙拉吧」就是其中一家最棒的。

　　如同它的名稱所暗示的，「沙拉吧」提供許多沙拉，每一樣都很美味。這裡也有很多三明治和新鮮果汁可以選擇。可供內用或外帶。

```
┌ ─ ─ ─ ─ ─ ─ ┐
│ 氣氛：不錯      │
│ 食物：可口      │
│ 服務：不錯      │
│ 價格：便宜      │
└ ─ ─ ─ ─ ─ ─ ┘
```

卡薩諾瓦

　　「卡薩諾瓦」幾年前是這個城市裡最時髦的餐廳之一，但再也不是了。理由很簡單：餐廳的老闆喬治‧布林克曼被他的成功給沖昏頭了。一開始，餐廳的吸引力是因為上菜的人都來頭不小，服務生可能是息影的電視明星或者上過新聞的人。在「卡薩諾瓦」的夜晚，有一部分的樂趣就在於一邊享用廚師的創意美饌，一邊和服務生聊

天。

　　然而，布林克曼犯了個大錯。就是當他把注意力集中在特殊服務人員時，卻喪失了對廚房該有的關注。如今，「卡薩諾瓦」提供的食物嚐起來像是罐頭食品，而服務生則像是從馬戲團中出來的怪咖。

> 氣氛：尚可
> 食物：差
> 服務：尚可
> 價格：略貴

 **Vocabulary**

review	評論；批評
extensive	延伸的；多方面的；廣博的
head	主要的
chef	廚師
simplicity	簡樸；單純；坦率
trendy	時髦的；時下流行的
patio	天井；室外的庭院
reservation	訂位

recommend	建議
blend	綜合；混合物
sample	體驗
salmon	鮭魚
curry	咖哩
lack	缺乏；缺少
match	相配
bump	撞到
imply	暗示，提示
made-to-order	訂做的
dine-in	在餐廳內用餐
take-out	(食物) 外帶
appeal	吸引力
tin can	罐頭

lure   引誘

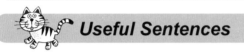 **Useful Sentences**

◎ Low-key 低調的

relaxed, enjoyable; though not exciting
放輕鬆的、令人享受的；不過較不刺激

A: How was your weekend?
你的週末過得如何？

B: It was pretty low-key. I just stayed home and watched TV.
相當平凡。我只是留在家裡看電視。

◎ From scratch 從頭開始

to do something by oneself from the very beginning of the task
從最初階段就親手做

A: I heard your computer crashed! Did you manage to save your essay?
我聽說你的電腦當機了。你有救回你的報告嗎？

B: No, I'm going to have to start writing it again from scratch.
沒有，我正要從頭開始寫。

◎ Spice up　添加風味

to make something spicier
使某事物更具有味道

A: This soup tastes pretty plain. Do you have anything to spice it up?
這湯喝起來十分平淡，你有什麼東西可以調味嗎？

B: Sure. There's some salt and pepper on the table.
有啊，桌上有一些鹽巴和胡椒。

◎ Go to one's head　沖昏頭了

to make somebody feel more important, more special, etc., than they really are
讓某人以為自己比實際情況更為重要、更特別……等

A: James keeps telling me how smart he is.
詹姆士不斷告訴我他有多聰明。

B: I know. He has really let that A he got in science class go to his head.
我了解。他真的被自然科拿到的那個 A 給沖昏頭了。

◎ Lose track of something 忘了某事

to forget about something that should be important
忘記重要的事

A: You're late! Where have you been?
你遲到了。你跑到哪裡去啦？

B: At the library. I lost track of time while I was doing my research.
我在圖書館。因為忙著做報告，就忘了時間了。

Test Yourself

1. Which of the following restaurants does The Travel Smart Guide to L.A. not recommend?
   A) Antoine's Italian Café   B) Zim Zim's
   C) The Salad Bar   D) Casa Nova

2. How is the food at Antoine's Italian Café?

    A) It is simple and fresh.   B) It is burnt in an oven.

    C) It is hot and spicy.   D) It is very expensive.

3. Which of the following items might one order at The Salad Bar?

    A) a hamburger and French fries

    B) a turkey sandwich and fresh orange juice

    C) pizza made in a wood-burning oven

    D) pacific salmon and Thai curry

4. Which of the following is not true?

    A) The food at Zim Zim's is very good.

    B) Zim Zim's is more expensive than The Salad Bar.

    C) The chef at Zim Zim's is David Chen.

    D) Zim Zim's is not often crowded.

5. Why would one not want to eat at Casa Nova?

    A) It is highly recommended by The Travel Smart Guide to L.A.

    B) The food there is served by interesting people.

    C) It is owned by a man named George Brinkman.

    D) Neither the food nor the service is very good.

 測驗題庫中譯

1. 下列哪個餐廳是「洛杉磯聰明旅遊指南」不推薦的？

A)「安東尼義大利餐館」 B)「齊齊」

C)「沙拉吧」 D)「卡薩諾瓦」

2.「安東尼義大利餐館」的食物怎麼樣？

A) 簡樸而新鮮 B) 用烤爐烘焙的

C) 又辛又辣 D) 相當貴

3. 下列哪個東西是可能在「沙拉吧」點到的？

A) 漢堡和新鮮薯條 B) 火雞三明治和新鮮柳橙汁

C) 用燒木頭的火爐烤的披薩 D) 太平洋鮭魚和泰式咖哩

4. 下列何者不對？

A)「齊齊」的食物很棒 B)「齊齊」比沙拉吧貴

C)「齊齊」的主廚是約翰・陳 D)「齊齊」通常都不擁擠

5. 為什麼有人不想在「卡薩諾瓦」用餐？

A) 因為「洛杉磯聰明旅遊指南」強烈推薦

B) 那裡由一些有趣的人服務上菜

C) 它的老闆是一個叫做喬治・布林克曼的男人

D) 食物和服務品質都不是很好

Unit 6 Lydia's Choice

Aunt June returns to the car after finishing her errands.

Aunt June : OK! I'm all done now. Have you made up your mind about what we'll be doing this afternoon?

Lydia : I think so. I'd like to check out the Hispanic district so that I can pick up some souvenirs for my friends and family back home. And even though I can't afford to buy anything at the designer boutiques, I'd really like to see Rodeo Drive.

Aunt June : That's the beauty of window shopping- it's free! How about lunch?

Lydia : I haven't decided on that yet. There are a couple of great restaurants listed in the guidebook, but I can't decide between them.

Aunt June : Well, how about I introduce you to one of my favorites? It's quite small, but the food is always delicious.

Lydia： That sounds perfect. What's it called?

Aunt Jane： It's called Olivier's. It's a French bistro.

Lydia： French food? You mean like frog's legs and snails?

Aunt June： (laughing) There are other things on the menu if those things don't appeal to you.

Lydia： That's a relief! I'm pretty hungry, but the sight of a pile of slimy things on my plate might have made me lose my appetite!

麗迪亞的選擇

茱兒阿姨在結束了差事後回到了車上。

茱兒阿姨： 好了，我完工了。你已經決定好我們今天下午要做什麼了嗎？

麗迪亞： 我想是的。我想去看看希斯佩尼克區，這樣我回家時可以選一些紀念品給朋友和家人。還有，雖然我

買不起設計師精品服飾店的任何東西，我還是想去
羅迪歐大街看看。

茱兒阿姨：　好就好在可以逛櫥窗──這是免費的。那午餐呢？

麗迪亞：　　我還沒決定好。導覽手冊上列了一大堆很棒的餐
廳，可以我很難從當中做出決定。

茱兒阿姨：　這樣啊，那讓我介紹一家我的最愛怎麼樣？是一家
蠻小的餐廳，不過食物很美味。

麗迪亞：　　聽起來很棒。叫什麼名字呢？

茱兒阿姨：　它叫做「奧莉薇」。是家法國小飯館。

麗迪亞：　　法國食物？你是說像是青蛙腿或者蝸牛之類的食物
嗎？

茱兒阿姨：　（笑著）如果這些東西無法吸引你的話，菜單上還
有其他食物。

麗迪亞：　　還好！我實在是很餓，但是如果看到一堆噁心的東
西在我的盤子上，我恐怕會食慾不佳。

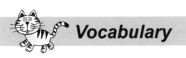 **Vocabulary**

bistro	小酒館；小飯館
snail	蝸牛
pile	一堆

slimy	黏糊糊的；惹人厭的
plate	盤子

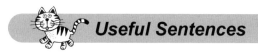 **Useful Sentences**

◎ That's the beauty of... **優點**

the good thing about something
某事物的美好部分

A: My car was stolen again last week. That's the third time this year that it's happened to me.
上禮拜我的車子又被偷了。這是今年第三次發生在我身上了。

B: That's the beauty of owning an old, ugly car like mine: no one ever wants to steal it!
這就是我家老舊爛車的好處了。從沒有人想要偷它。

◎ Lose one's appetite **食慾不振**

to feel that one is no longer hungry because of something one has seen or heard.
由於看到或聽到的某樣事物，使人失去胃口

A: Why aren't you eating? I thought you were hungry.
你為什麼不吃了？我以為你很餓。

B: I was until I saw the man at that table over there put his finger in his nose. Now I've lost my appetite!

我是很餓，不過看到那桌的男人把手指伸進鼻孔裡，我就完全沒有食慾了。

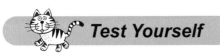 **Test Yourself**

1. Where does Lydia want to go to buy souvenirs?

    A) The Hispanic district   B) Rodeo Drive

    C) Olivier's   D) The window shop

2. What kind of restaurant is Olivier's?

    A) an Italian one   B) a French one

    C) a Mexican one   D) a Chinese one

3. What does Lydia think that frog's legs and snails would be like?

    A) delicious   B) expensive

    C) interesting   D) slimy

4. Why won't Lydia have to eat frog's legs?

    A) Her aunt won't allow it.

    B) There are other things to eat at Olivier's.

C) Oliver's doesn't serve them.

D) Lydia will eat snails instead.

5. How would seeing frog's legs on her plate make Lydia feel?

    A) excited   B) tempted

    C) disgusted   D) sleepy

 測驗題庫中譯

1. 麗迪亞想去哪裡買紀念品呢？

    A) 希斯佩尼克區   B) 羅迪歐大街   C)「奧莉薇」   D) 樹窗商店

2.「奧莉薇」是哪種餐廳？

    A) 義大利   B) 法國   C) 墨西哥   D) 中國

3. 麗迪亞認為青蛙腿和蝸牛看起來怎麼樣？

    A) 很美味   B) 很貴   C) 有趣   D) 令人噁心的

4. 為什麼麗迪亞不必吃青蛙腿？

    A) 她的阿姨不准她吃   B)「奧莉薇」有其他東西可以點

    C)「奧莉薇」不供應青蛙腿   D) 麗迪亞想吃蝸牛

5. 倘若麗迪亞看到青蛙腿在她的盤子裡面，她會覺得怎樣？

    A) 興奮   B) 想吃它   C) 噁心   D) 想睡覺

Chapter 5
An End-of-Sum mer Barbecue
夏末 BBQ

Unit 1 Email from Lydia

Dear Meg,

How's it hanging?! I've been in L.A. now for almost three months, and I've learned so much. My English is better, and I've found out a lot about American culture. I'm looking forward to coming home in a couple of weeks, but I will miss everyone here so much.

Next weekend my Aunt and Uncle are throwing a farewell party for me. They said that I can invite all of the friends that I have made since coming to L.A.- I must admit, that's quite a few! From my classmates at English school, to friends I've met through my cousin Eric, to kids my age in the neighborhood, I'll probably end up inviting thirty people! I hope that Aunt June and Uncle George won't mind!

Actually, there's one person in particular who I'm hoping to invite to my party: a boy named Will. He is one of my classmates from English school, and he's really cute. I've had a crush on him all summer, but I don't think he knows. Will is from Japan, so the only way we've been able to talk is in English. Let me tell you, this has been a great incentive for me to study harder! I hope that Will wants to come to the party, and then I can ask him for his email address. It is my hope that, even though we'll be far apart when the summer is over, we can still keep in touch through the Internet — just as I have kept in touch with you and all of my friends back at home.

Miss you lots!

Love,

Lydia

P.S. You are never on ICQ anymore. Why not?

麗迪亞的電子信件

親愛的梅格,最近如何?

我已經在洛杉磯待了將近三個月了,並且學到很多東西。

我的英文有進步了,並且了解到許多美國的文化。我很期待兩個禮拜後就可以回家,但我也會非常想念在這裡的每一個人。

下週末我阿姨和姨丈會為我舉辦告別派對,他們說我可以邀請所有我來到洛杉磯之後認識的朋友——我得承認,實在是不少。有我在英語學校的同班同學、透過我表哥艾瑞克認識的朋友、還有鄰近地區跟我同年齡相彷的人,我很可能最後會邀請到三十個人。我希望茱兒阿姨和喬治姨丈不會介意。

事實上，有一個人是我特別想邀請來派對的：一個叫做威爾的男孩。他是我在英語學校的一個同學，他真的非常可愛。整個夏天我一直都迷戀著他，可是我想他不知道。威爾來自日本，所以我們唯一能夠溝通的語言就是英文。偷偷告訴你吧，這是使我更努力學習的重要誘因。我希望威爾會想來參加派對，這樣我就可以問他的電子信箱了。我希望，即使夏天結束後我們會分開，我們依舊能夠透過網路保持聯絡，就像我一直和你以及所有在家鄉的朋友保持聯絡一樣。

很想你！

愛你的麗迪亞

PS 妳一直沒出現在 ICQ 上，為什麼呢？

Vocabulary

culture	文化
farewell	再見；告別
in particular	特別是
incentive	刺激物；誘因
keep in touch	保持聯絡

 *Useful Sentences*

◎ How's it hanging? 最近怎樣？

(informal expression) How are you?
（非正式用法）你好嗎？

A: Long time no see, Kim! How's it hanging?
好久不見，金！最近怎樣？

B: Pretty good, thanks!
很好，謝謝！

◎ Throw a party 辦舞會

to have a party
舉行派對

A: I heard that Paul is throwing a party to celebrate turning thirty!
我聽說保羅要舉行一個慶祝三十歲生日的派對。

B: Really? I wonder if I'll be invited.
真的嗎？不知道我會不會被邀請。

◎ Have a crush on somebody　暗戀

to like somebody in a romantic way
以浪漫的方式喜歡著某人

A：I think that Ray has a crush on Mary.
我想雷迷上了瑪麗。

B：Me too! He always looks at her when she walks by, and won't stop talking about her.
我也這麼覺得。當她經過時，他總是盯著她看，而且不停地談論有關她的事情。

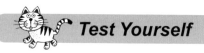 **Test Yourself**

1. Why will Aunt June and Uncle George throw a party?
   A) because Lydia's birthday is coming
   B) because Lydia has just arrived in L.A.
   C) because Lydia is going home soon
   D) because Lydia's anniversary is coming

2. Who will Lydia invite to her party?
   A) her friends and classmates
   B) her friends from Taiwan and China

C) only a boy named Will

D) only Eric's friends

3. Which of the following statements is false?

   A) Will is from Japan.

   B) Lydia thinks Will is cute.

   C) Will can speak Chinese.

   D) Lydia wants to invite Will to her party.

4. What has given Lydia a reason to study harder?

   A) The fact that she wants to live in America forever.

   B) The fact that her aunt and uncle put a lot of pressure on her.

   C) The fact that she must leave America soon.

   D) The fact that English is the language she must use to communicate with Will.

5. When will the party be?

   A) after Lydia leaves   B) in a few hours

   C) in about a week   D) in a couple of weeks

 測驗題庫中譯

1. 為什麼茱兒阿姨和喬治姨丈要舉辦派對？

　　A) 因為麗迪亞的生日快到了　　B) 因為麗迪亞剛到洛杉磯

　　C) 很為麗迪亞很快就要回家了　　D) 因為麗迪亞的結婚紀念日要到了

2. 麗迪亞會邀請誰來參加派對？

　　A) 她的朋友和同班同學　　B) 來自台灣和中國的朋友

　　C) 只有一個叫做威爾的男孩　　D) 只有艾瑞克的朋友

3. 下列哪個敘述錯誤？

　　A) 威爾來自日本

　　B) 麗迪亞認為威爾很可愛

　　C) 威爾會說中國話

　　D) 麗迪亞想邀請威爾參加她的派對

4. 什麼原因促使麗迪亞更努力學習？

　　A) 因為她想永遠住在美國

　　B) 因為她的阿姨和姨丈給她很大的壓力

　　C) 因為她必定很快就會離開美國了

　　D) 因為英語是她跟威爾溝通的語言

5. 派對在何時舉行？

　　A) 麗迪亞離開後　　B) 幾個小時內後

　　C) 大約一個禮拜內後　　D) 兩個禮拜後

MP3-30

Invitations

Lydia comes into the kitchen and finds her Uncle George sitting at the table.

Uncle George : Speak of the Devil! I was just on the phone with your Aunt June, and we were discussing your farewell party.

Lydia : Oh?

Uncle George : We were wondering if you'd decided what kind of party you'd like?

Lydia : Well, I was thinking that we could have a barbecue in the backyard.

Uncle George : You know, you could make it a pool party.

Lydia : That's what I was thinking. I'll ask everyone to bring their bathing suits and those who want to go swimming, can.

Uncle George : That's a fine plan.

Lydia :　　　　　Yep, the backyard should be perfect. There's a lot of space out there, so there will be room for all my friends.

Uncle George :　Just how many people were you planning on inviting?

Lydia :　　　　　Well, there are my friends from school, the people I've met through Eric, the neighbors...

Uncle George :　That sounds like quite a crowd- but the more the merrier! Have you
invited anyone yet?

Lydia :　　　　　No, not yet. I just finished making the invitations that I'll give out to let people know about the party.

Uncle George :　Mind if I take a look?

Lydia :　　　　　Not at all! In fact, this one is for you!

Pool Party and Barbecue!

You're invited to a party to celebrate Lydia Hsu's summer in L.A.
There'll be plenty of food, games, and fun.
We hope that you can make it!

Date: August 20
Time: 4 pm
Where: 1873 Milton court, L.A.
What to bring: bathing suit & towel
RSVP: 555-8434

邀請

麗迪亞走進到廚房並看到坐在桌子前面的喬治姨丈。

喬治姨丈： 説曹操曹操就到！我剛剛正在和妳茱兒阿姨講電話，我們在討論妳的告別派對。

麗迪亞： 怎麼樣呢？

喬治姨丈： 我們在想是否讓妳決定想舉辦什麼類型的派對？

麗迪亞： 嗯，我想我們可以在後院烤肉。

喬治姨丈： 你知道的，你可以舉辦個游泳池畔派對。

麗迪亞： 那正也是我所想的。我希望每個人帶著他們的游泳

裝備，這樣想游泳的人就可以游泳了。

喬治姨丈： 這是個好主意。

麗迪亞： 太好了，那後院就是太完美的地點了。那裡的空間很大，可以容納我所有的朋友。

喬治姨丈： 那你準備邀請多少人來呢？

麗迪亞： 這個，有我學校的同學、透過艾瑞克認識的朋友，還有鄰居……

喬治姨丈： 聽起來很多，不過人越多越熱鬧。妳已經邀請任何人了嗎？

麗迪亞： 還沒，我才剛做好邀請函，晚點才會發出去給大家。

喬治姨丈： 妳介意我看看嗎？

麗迪亞： 一點也不，其實這張就是給你的。

游泳池畔烤肉派對

您受邀參加此派對，歡送麗迪亞·許在洛杉磯的夏天。

屆時將有許多食物、遊戲及趣味。

希望您能參加！

日期：八月二十日

時間：下午四點

地點：洛杉磯，彌爾頓巷，1873 號

攜帶物品：泳裝和毛巾

敬請答覆：555-8434

 **Vocabulary**

discuss	討論
bathing suit	泳裝
room for	提供的空間
celebrate	慶祝
plenty	很多的，大量的
towel	毛巾
RSVP	敬請答覆（源自法語＝répondez s'il vous plaît）

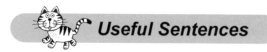

Useful Sentences

◎ Speak of the devil 說人人到

used when one sees somebody that they have just been talking about
指才剛講完，話題人物就出現了

A: My sister is going to study abroad next summer.
我妹妹明年夏天要出國唸書了。

B: Speak of the devil! Here comes your sister now!
說人人到！妳妹妹來了！

◎ Meet through 如何認識

used to tell how somebody knows another person
用以說明某人如何認識另一個人

A: How did you meet your husband?
妳怎麼認識妳先生的？

B: We met through our employer: we're co-workers!
我們是透過我們的老闆認識的：我們是同事。

◎ The more the merrier 人愈多愈快樂

the more people there are, the more fun there will be
有越多的人，氣氛就越歡樂

A: My brother wants to come with us to the movies.
我弟弟想跟我們一起去看電影。

B: Great! The more the merrier!
好啊！人越多越熱鬧。

◎ Make it 到達

to go to a prearranged occasion
到達一個事先安排到的場合

A: Will you be able to make it to the wedding?
可以來參加婚禮嗎？

B: Of course! I wouldn't miss it for the world!
當然，我絕對不會錯過的。

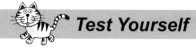 **Test Yourself**

1. Who was Uncle George just talking about?

   A) Aunt June   B) Eric

   C) Lydia   D) The devil

2. What should guests to Lydia's party bring?

   A) presents for Lydia

   B) food to barbecue

   C) bathing suits for swimming

   D) invitations to the party

3. Where will the party take place?

   A) in the backyard   B) at Uncle George's office

   C) on Rodeo Drive   D) in the Hispanic district

4. When will the party start?

   A) in the morning   B) at noon

   C) in the afternoon   D) at night

5. Who is the first person to get an invitation to Lydia's party?

   A) Uncle George   B) Aunt June

   C) Meg   D) Will

測驗題庫中譯

1. 喬治姨丈剛剛談論到誰？

    A) 茱兒阿姨   B) 艾瑞克   C) 麗迪亞   D) 魔鬼

2. 參加麗迪亞派對的人應該帶什麼東西？

    A) 給麗迪亞的禮物   B) 烤肉的食物

    C) 游泳的裝備   D) 參加派對的邀請函

3. 派對在哪裡舉行？

    A) 在後院   B) 在喬治姨丈的辦公室

    C) 在羅迪歐大街   D) 在希斯佩尼克區

4. 派對何時開始？

    A) 在早上   B) 在中午   C) 在下午   D) 在晚上

5. 誰第一個收到麗迪亞的派對邀請函？

    A) 喬治姨丈   B) 茱兒阿姨   C) 梅格   D) 威爾

Unit 3 — Instant Messaging

While Lydia has been in L.A., she has kept in touch with her friends back home through emails and through instant messages. She uses ICQ. Today she is on ICQ, and she sees that her good friend Meg is on, too.

Lyd168: Meg! Finally ;)

Coolgrl: Sorry I haven't been on in a while. I took a trip.

Lyd168: Oh, yeah! I forgot you were going away.

Coolgrl: I guess you're too caught up in you L.A. life... I hear there are lots of hot guys there. LOL

Lyd168: So you did get my email!

Coolgrl: Yes! Will sounds nice. Will he be at your party?

Lyd168: I think so. I gave out invitations to my classmates yesterday, and he said he'd try to make it.

Coolgrl: Cool.

Lyd168:   How's your summer going anyway?

Coolgrl: Not too shabby! Europe was fun.

Lyd168:   Where'd you go?

Coolgrl: Paris, Lisbon, and Rome. It was a
two-week group tour.

Lyd168:   Sounds like a lot of ground to cover in
just two weeks!

Coolgrl: It was. That was the only downside of
the trip. There was no time to relax. We
were always on the move.

Lyd168:   Well, you've got all the time in the
world to relax now.

Coolgrl: No, I haven't! You must not have
heard!

Lyd168:   Heard what?

Coolgrl: I got a job at 7-ELEVEN. I'll be
working there until school starts!

即時訊息

當麗迪亞在洛杉磯時，她一直都透過電子郵件和即時訊息
和家鄉的朋友保持聯繫。她使用的系統是 ICQ。今天她在 ICQ
上，而她看到她的朋友梅格也在上面。

Lyd168： 梅格，終於遇到你了。

Coolgrl： 很抱歉我有一陣子沒上來了，我去旅行了。

Lyd168： 喔，對啦，我忘了妳不在家。

Coolgrl： 我想妳很醉心於在洛杉磯的生活……我聽說那裡有很多很棒的男孩。哈一哈

Lyd168： 妳已經收到我的電子郵件了！

Coolgrl： 是啊，威爾聽起來很棒，他會去妳的派對嗎？

Lyd168： 我想會吧，我昨天把邀請函發給我的同學了，他說他會抽空參加。

Coolgrl： 太好了。

Lyd168： 妳的暑假過得怎樣？

Coolgrl： 還不賴。歐洲很有意思。

Lyd168： 妳去了哪些地方？

Coolgrl： 巴黎、里斯本和羅馬，是兩個星期的旅行團。

Lyd168： 聽起來兩個禮拜之內要去很多地方。

Coolgrl： 是啊，那是旅行當中唯一的缺點。沒有時間放鬆，總是一直在前進。

Lyd168： 這個嘛，現在妳有一大堆時間可以休息啦。

Coolgrl： 才還沒有呢。妳一定還沒聽說！

Lyd168： 聽說什麼？

Coolgrl： 我在 7-ELEVEN 找到一份工作，開學前我都要在那兒工作。

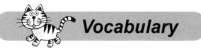
Vocabulary

instant message	即時信息
screen name	使用者暱稱
dialogue	對話
hot	熱情的
LOL (laugh out loud)	大笑出來
shabby	破爛的；邋遢的
group tour	旅行團
cover	包含；包括
downside	不利；壞處

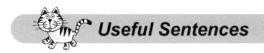

Useful Sentences

◎ Be caught up in something **著迷於某事**

to pay so much attention to something that one forgets about other things
因為太過專注於某事物而忘記其他事情

A: Can I talk to you for a minute?
我可以跟你談一下嗎？

B: Can't you wait? I'm really caught up in this movie on TV.
可以等一下嗎？我實在無法從這部電視影片中抽身。

◎ Be on the move **持續移動**

to be busy; to go from place to place without rest
很忙碌；從一個地方到另一個地方，從未休息

A: Are you sure you want a job working as a flight attendant? You'll always be on the move.
你確定你想要當空服員？那樣你會一直很忙碌喔。

B: That's what I'm looking forward to most! A life of travel!
那正是我最渴求的！旅遊的生活！

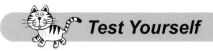

Test Yourself

1. How are Meg and Lydia communicating?

   A) by the telephone   B) by mail

   C) by instant messages   D) by talking face to face

2. What is Lydia's screen name?

   A) Coolgrl   B) Lyd168

   C) Lydia   D) Meg

3. Where has Meg been lately?

   A) Europe   B) America

   C) Africa   D) Antarctica

4. What does Lydia tell Meg about Will?

   A) He is her boyfriend.

   B) He is no longer her friend.

   C) He is coming to her party.

   D) He is leaving school.

5. Why won't Meg have much free time until school starts?

   A) She must go to summer school.

   B) She will be traveling abroad.

C) She is sick with a cold.

D) She got a job.

 測驗題庫中譯

1. 梅格和麗迪亞如何溝通？

　　A) 透過電話　　　　　　　　B) 透過信件

　　C) 透過即時訊息　　　　　　D) 面對面談話

2. 麗迪亞的使用者代號是什麼？

　　A) Coolgrl　　　B) Lyd168　　　C) 麗迪亞　　　D) 梅格

3. 梅格最近去了哪裡？

　　A) 歐洲　　　　　B) 美國　　　　C) 非洲　　　　D) 南極洲

4. 麗迪亞跟梅格說了什麼有關威爾的事情？

　　A) 他是她男朋友　　　　　　B) 他再也不是她的朋友了

　　C) 他會參加她的派對　　　　D) 他要離開學校了

5. 為什麼在開學前梅格沒有太多休閒時間？

　　A) 她得上暑期課程　　　　　B) 她要出國旅行了

　　C) 她因為感冒而不舒服　　　D) 她有了工作

Unit 4 · Food for the Party

It's Wednesday, and Eric and Lydia are talking in the kitchen.

Eric : So, have you passed out all of the invitations to your farewell party yet?

Lydia : Almost. I still have to give one to our neighbor, Mr. Smith.

Eric : Has everyone RSVP-ed?

Lydia : No. I still haven't heard from a couple of my classmates. They're not sure if they can make it. But my fingers are crossed that they can come.

Eric : Well, maybe you can persuade them by giving them a hint about what's on the menu! What are you planning on serving?

Lydia : Barbecued hamburgers and hotdogs, of course...

Eric : Yum!

Lydia : Potato salad, corn on the cob...

Eric : My mouth is watering!

Lydia : Fruit punch and iced tea to drink...

Eric : And for dessert?

Lydia : Hmm. I hadn't thought about dessert.

Eric : How about brownies?

Lydia : But I don't know how to make brownies!

Eric : It's as easy as pie. I make them all the time — I'll write down the recipe for you!

Lydia : Thanks, Eric!

Eric : Hey, what are cousins for?

派對食物

今天是星期三，艾瑞克和麗迪亞在廚房聊天說話。

艾瑞克： 那麼，你已經把所有妳的告別派對邀請函都發出去嗎？

麗迪亞： 大部分都發了。其中還有一張要給我們的鄰居，史密斯先生。

艾瑞克： 所有的人都答覆了嗎？

麗迪亞： 沒有。我還沒接到我的兩個同班同學的通知。他們還不確定是否能來。不過我祈禱他們可以參加。

艾瑞克： 這個嘛，也許你可以給他們一點暗示，用派對上的食物說服他們來。妳要準備什麼吃的東西呢？

麗迪亞： 當然有烤肉漢堡和熱狗！

艾瑞克： 好棒！

麗迪亞： 馬鈴薯沙拉、玉蜀黍串……

艾瑞克： 我在流口水了。

麗迪亞： 飲料有水果酒和冰紅茶……

艾瑞克： 甜點呢？

麗迪亞： 嗯，我還沒想好甜點。

艾瑞克： 布朗尼巧克力蛋糕怎麼樣？

麗迪亞： 可是我不會做布朗尼巧克力蛋糕。

艾瑞克： 很簡單。我一天到晚都在做，我會可以把製作方法寫給妳。

麗迪亞： 謝謝你，艾瑞克。

艾瑞克： 嘿，表哥是用來幹什麼的？

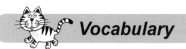 **Vocabulary**

pass out	分發出去
persuade	說服；勸說
hint	暗示；提示
potato	馬鈴薯

corn on the cob	玉蜀黍串
fruit punch	水果酒
iced tea	冰紅茶
dessert	甜點；點心
brownies	布朗尼巧克力蛋糕
recipe	製作方法；訣竅；配方；食譜

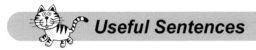 **Useful Sentences**

◎ Cross one's fingers　祈禱

To hope for something
期待某事物

A: Oh! It's almost time for the lottery numbers to be picked.
喔！樂透號碼開獎的時間快到了。

B: I've got my fingers crossed that we'll win the big prize!
我一直在祈禱我們可以贏得大獎。

◎ One's mouth is watering　嘴巴在流口水

to feel very hungry in anticipation of something delicious
渴望某個美味的食物而感到非常飢餓

A: Look at all the ice cream in this store. There must be fifty different flavors.
看看這家店所有的冰淇淋，絕對有五十種不同的口味。

B: My mouth is watering! Let's buy some!
我在流口水了！我們買一些吃吧。

◎ As easy as pie 小事一樁

to be very easy to do
非常容易做

A: This math problem is so difficult.
這個數學問題好難。

B: No it's not. Here, I'll show you how to do it. It'll be as easy as pie!
才不會。我告訴你怎麼做，它相當容易。

Test Yourself

1 Who does Lydia still need to invite to her party?

A) one of her classmates   B) someone in the family

C) a neighbor   D) a co-worker

2. Which of the following is not a kind of food Lydia will serve at her party?

A) hamburgers   B) corn

C) brownies   D) tomatoes

3. How does Eric feel about the food Lydia is planning on serving?

    A) He thinks it will be delicious.

    B) He's worried few people will like it.

    C) He knows that he won't eat it.

    D) He believes it will ruin the party.

4. What will Lydia serve her guests to drink?

    A) soda and water   B) beer and wine

    C) fruit punch and iced tea   D) hot tea and coffee

5. How will Lydia know how to make brownies?

    A) Eric will give her a recipe.

    B) She will find a recipe on the Internet.

    C) Aunt June will show her how to do it.

    D) She will ask a baker for instructions.

測驗題庫中譯

1. 麗迪亞還要邀請誰參加派對？

    A) 其中一個同班同學   B) 家裡的某一個人

    C) 一個鄰居   D) 一個同事

2. 下列何種食物不是麗迪亞要在派對上供應的？

    A) 漢堡   B) 玉米

    C) 布朗尼巧克力蛋糕   D) 蕃茄

3. 艾瑞克對於麗迪亞準備要提供的食物有什麼感覺？

    A) 他覺得會相當好吃   B) 他擔心沒什麼人會喜歡

    C) 他知道他不會吃   D) 他認為它們會毀了派對

4. 麗迪亞要請他的客人喝什麼？

    A) 汽水和開水   B) 啤酒和葡萄酒

    C) 水果酒和冰紅茶   D) 熱茶和咖啡

5. 麗迪亞怎麼知道如何做布朗尼巧克力蛋糕？

    A) 艾瑞克會給她製作方法   B) 她會在網路上找製作方法

    C) 茱兒阿姨會做給她看   D) 她會請教一個烘焙師

Unit 5 · Recipes

Lots of people will be coming to the barbecue in the backyard, so Lydia and Aunt June are in the kitchen preparing food to eat. They have the hamburger patties and hotdogs on a tray in the fridge so that later Uncle George can cook them on the barbecue. Lydia has just made fruit punch, and Aunt June has finished the potato salad. Now they are going to make brownies.

To make the food, Aunt June and Lydia follow recipes in Aunt June's favorite cookbook— except for the brownies, because those were Eric's idea!

New Potato Salad:

Ingredients

20 medium-sized new potatoes, boiled
5 celery stalks, chopped
1 Spanish onion, diced
1/2 cup Dijon mustard
1/4 cup olive oil
pinch of salt & pepper to taste

Directions

1. In bowl, blend Dijon mustard and oil thoroughly.
2. Boil potatoes with skins until soft. Drain water and allow to cool.
3. Cut potatoes into small pieces.
4. Put potatoes in bowl. Add celery, onion, and dressing.
5. Cover and chill in refrigerator for several hours.

Serves 12

Easy Brownies

Ingredients

1/4 cup flour
1/2 cup butter
1/2 cup cocoa powder
1/2 cup white sugar
two eggs
1/2 cup walnuts

Directions

1. Preheat oven to 375 degrees.
2. In a sauce pan, melt butter on stove. Add cocoa powder and sugar. Stir until mixed; allow to cool.
3. Stir in eggs and flour.
4. Pour mixture into baking pan.
5. Bake for 20 minutes.
6. Cool before serving

Serves 6

食譜

很多人會到後院來參加烤肉，所以麗迪亞和茱兒阿姨正在廚房準備要吃的食物。他們的冰箱裡面有個放著做漢堡用的小圓餅以及一盤熱狗的盤子，這樣晚一點喬治姨丈就可以在烤肉派對時烤了。麗迪亞剛做好水果酒，茱兒阿姨則做好了馬鈴薯沙拉。現在他們要做布朗尼巧克力蛋糕了。

為了準備食物，茱兒阿姨和麗迪亞參照著茱兒阿姨最喜歡的食譜書的做法——除了布朗尼巧克力蛋糕除外，因為那是艾瑞克的主意！

新鮮馬鈴薯沙拉

材料：

二十個中型新鮮馬鈴薯，煮熟

五棵芹菜莖，剁碎

一顆西班牙洋蔥，切丁

二分之一杯法國第戎芥茉

四分之一杯橄欖油

少許調味用的鹽及胡椒

做法：

1. 在碗中將法國第戎芥茉和橄欖油在碗中充分混合。

2. 馬鈴薯連皮一起煮至軟熟，瀝乾置涼。

3. 馬鈴薯切成薄片狀。

4. 馬鈴薯放進碗中，加入芹菜、洋蔥及調味料。

5. 加蓋，放入冰箱冷藏數小時。

十二人份

簡易布朗尼巧克力蛋糕

材料：

四分之一杯麵粉

二分之一杯奶油

二分之一杯可可粉

二分之一杯白糖

兩顆雞蛋

二分之一杯核桃

做法：

1. 預熱烤爐至三百七十五度。

2. 平底鍋置於爐火上，將奶油融化。加入可可粉及白糖，攪拌調勻；置涼。

3. 加入雞蛋和麵粉混合攪拌。

4. 將混合物倒進烤鍋。

5. 烘烤二十分鐘。

6. 待置涼後即可食用。

六人份

 **Vocabulary**

prepare	準備
hamburger patty	漢堡小圓餅
tray	盤子；托盤
cookbook	食譜
boil	煮沸
chop	砍；剁碎

dice	切丁；骰子
celery stalk	芹菜莖
new potato	新鮮馬鈴薯
dijon mustard	法國第戎芥末
blend	混合
thoroughly	徹底地；完全地
dressing	調味醬料
chill	使變冷
cocoa powder	可可粉
stir	攪拌
walnuts	核桃
preheat	預先加熱
baking pan	烤鍋

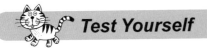

Test Yourself

1. Which of the following is not an ingredient in the new potato salad recipe?

   A) oil   B) mustard

   C) salt   D) sugar

2. How much potato salad will the recipe make?

   A) enough for Aunt June

   B) enough for six people

   C) enough for twelve people

   D) enough for twenty people

3. If 36 people are at the barbecue, how many eggs will Lydia need to use in order to make sure there are enough brownies for everyone?

   A) two   B) twelve

   C) twenty   D) two-hundred

4. How long will the brownies need to be in the oven?

   A) ten minutes   B) fifteen minutes

   C) twenty minutes   D) twenty-five minutes

5. Before eating the brownies, what should happen?

A) They should be chopped.

B) They should be cooled.

C) They should be covered.

D) They should be diced.

 測驗題庫中譯

1. 下列何者不是製作新鮮馬鈴薯沙拉的材料？

　A) 油　　　　B) 芥茉　　　C) 鹽巴　　　D) 糖

2. 馬鈴薯沙拉的食譜是幾人份？

　A) 茱兒阿姨的份　B) 六人份　　C) 十二人份　D) 二十人份

3. 如果烤肉派對上有三十六個人，麗迪亞需要多少雞蛋才能做出足夠份量的布朗尼蛋糕？

　A) 兩個　　　　B) 十二個　　C) 二十個　　D) 二百個

4. 布朗尼蛋糕需要在烤箱中烤多久？

　A) 十分鐘　　　B) 十五分鐘　C) 二十分鐘　D) 二十五分鐘

5. 在吃布朗尼蛋糕之前，應該先做什麼？

　A) 切碎　　　　B) 置涼　　　C) 加蓋　　　D) 切丁

Unit 6 Barbecue in the Backyard

It's six o'clock and the barbecue is in full swing. Some people are swimming in the pool, some people are playing a game of croquet, and some are sipping iced tea on the patio and chatting.

Uncle George has started the barbecue, and is going into the house to get the tray of meat from the fridge. He has kept it there until now for two reasons: the first is that he knows if the meat isn't cool, then bacteria can grow on it and make it dangerous to eat; the second is because he has noticed the neighbor's dog in the backyard. Uncle George knows that if it sees the meat unattended, it will help itself!

Aunt June is also in the kitchen. She is busy making more fruit punch because the first batch is gone!

Eric is getting out of the pool right now. He can tell that his dad is getting ready to barbecue, and he wants to be first in line for a hamburger. As usual, Eric is very hungry!

Lydia is in the backyard, too, drinking iced tea and chatting with one of her friends. Can you guess who?

It's Will, the boy she has a crush on. It turns out that he has a crush on her, too!

"This has been the perfect summer," Lydia thinks to herself. "I'm sure going to miss everyone in L.A.!"

後院的烤肉派對

已經六點了,烤肉派對正火熱地進行著。有些人在池裡游泳,有些人在玩槌球比賽,還有些人在天井啜飲著冰茶、聊著天。

喬治姨丈已經開始烤東西了,他正要到屋裡把冰箱裡面裝盤的肉拿出來。有兩個原因讓他一直把肉放在冰箱裡:其一是他知道如果肉沒有冷藏的話,就會滋生細菌,使肉的品質不安全;其二是他注意到鄰居的狗也在後院。喬治姨丈知道,如果狗發現沒人注意就會把肉吃掉。

茱兒阿姨也在廚房裡面。她正忙著做更多的水果酒,因為第一批已經喝完了。

艾瑞克正從游泳池出來。他知道他爸爸已經準備要開始烤肉了,他想要第一個拿到漢堡。如同往常一樣,艾瑞克非常餓。

麗迪亞也在後院,她正喝著冰紅茶並且跟她的一個朋友聊天。猜得到是誰嗎?是威爾,那個她迷戀已久的男孩。結果似乎是他也愛上她了。

「這真是個完美的夏天。」麗迪亞想著,「我確信我一定會想念在洛杉磯的每一個人!」

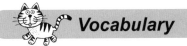
Vocabulary

croquet	槌球遊戲
sip	啜飲
bacteria	細菌
unattended	無人照管的
batch	一爐；一團；一組；一束

 **Useful Sentences**

◎ In full swing 高潮

for a party, event, or celebration to be well under way
派對、競賽、或者慶祝典禮順利進行

A: I wonder if anyone will notice that we're late for the party.
不知道有沒有人發現我們遲到了。

B: Probably not. By now, it's in full swing, and people will be having too much fun to notice whether or not we're there.
應該沒有吧。這個時刻，宴會正熱鬧著，大家正玩得開心，根本無暇注意我們到了沒。

◎ Help oneself 自己取用

to get something by oneself
自己拿取某件東西

A: May I have another cookie?
我可以再吃一塊餅乾嗎？

B: Of course! There are plenty in the jar. Just help yourself!
當然，罐子裡有很多，請自便吧。

 **Test Yourself**

1. Who is Lydia talking to?

    A) Will   B) Eric

    C) Aunt June   D) Uncle George

2. What is Eric doing?

    A) playing Baseball   B) barbecuing hamburgers

    C) helping his parents   D) getting out of the pool

3. What is Aunt June making?

    A) hamburgers   B) iced tea

    C) fruit punch   D) potato salad

4. Where is the tray of meat?

    A) in the dog's mouth   B) on the barbecue

    C) in the pool   D) in the fridge

5. Who is not thinking about food right now?

    A) Lydia   B) Eric

    C) Aunt June   D) Uncle George

 測驗題庫中譯

1. 麗迪亞在跟誰說話？

A) 威爾

B) 艾瑞克

C) 茱兒阿姨

D) 喬治姨丈

2. 艾瑞克在做什麼？

A) 打棒球

B) 烤漢堡

C) 幫忙他的父母

D) 從水池出來

3. 茱兒阿姨在做什麼？

A) 漢堡

B) 冰紅茶

C) 水果酒

D) 馬鈴薯沙拉

4. 裝盤的肉放在哪裡？

A) 在狗的嘴巴裡

B) 在烤肉架上

C) 在水池裡面

D) 在冰箱裡面

5. 誰此時此刻想的不是食物？

A) 麗迪亞

B) 艾瑞克

C) 茱兒阿姨

D) 喬治姨丈

Answers 解答

Chapter ❶ Meet Lydia!

Unit 1	1. A	2. C	3. B	4. C	5. A
Unit 2	1. B	2. A	3. B	4. D	5. C
Unit 3	1. A	2. C	3. A	4. B	5. B
Unit 4	1. B	2. C	3. A	4. A	5. C
Unit 5	1. D	2. B	3. D	4. A	5. D
Unit 6	1. D	2. B	3. A	4. A	5. D
Unit 7	1. A	2. D	3. A	4. D	5. B
Unit 8	1. C	2. C	3. A	4. B	5. A

Chapter ❷ All About Eric

Unit 1	1. B	2. B	3. D	4. D	5. A
Unit 2	1. B	2. A	3. C	4. A	5. D
Unit 3	1. D	2. B	3. D	4. C	5. A
Unit 4	1. C	2. D	3. A	4. A	5. C
Unit 5	1. B	2. A	3. C	4. B	5. D
Unit 6	1. A	2. B	3. A	4. B	5. D
Unit 7	1. C	2. B	3. B	4. D	5. A

Chapter ❸ Uncle George's Day

Unit 1	1. B	2. C	3. D	4. C	5. A
Unit 2	1. A	2. C	3. A	4. D	5. D
Unit 3	1. A	2. C	3. A	4. C	5. C
Unit 4	1. B	2. C	3. C	4. A	5. D
Unit 5	1. B	2. A	3. D	4. A	5. C
Unit 6	1. D	2. D	3. A	4. C	5. D

Chapter ❹ Aunt June

Unit 1	1. B	2. D	3. A	4. B	5. C
	6. A	7. A	8. C	9. C	10. B
Unit 2	1.A	2. B	3. B	4. A	5. D
Unit 3	1. A	2. B	3. D	4. B	5. C
	6. B	7. C	8. D	9. C	10. A
Unit 4	1. A	2. B	3. B	4. C	5. B
Unit 5	1. D	2. B	3. B	4. D	5. D
Unit 6	1. A	2. B	3. D	4. B	5. C

Chapter ❺ Email from Lydia

Unit 1	1. C	2. A	3. C	4. D	5. C
Unit 2	1. C	2. C	3. A	4. C	5. A
Unit 3	1. C	2. B	3. A	4. A	5. D
Unit 4	1. C	2. D	3. A	4. C	5. A
Unit 5	1. B	2. C	3. B	4. C	5. B
Unit 6	1. A	2. D	3. C	4. D	5. A

MEMO

國家圖書館出版品預行編目資料

可以馬上學會的 超強英語閱讀課 / 蘇盈盈,
珊朵拉合著. -- 新北市：哈福企業, 2020.10

面；　公分. --（英語系列；66）

ISBN 978-986-99161-5-8(平裝附光碟片)
1.英語 2.讀本

805.18　　　　　　　　109014900

英語系列：66

書名 / 可以馬上學會的 超強英語閱讀課
合著 / 蘇盈盈‧珊朵拉
出版單位 / 哈福企業有限公司
責任編輯 / Mary Chang
封面設計 / Lin Lin House
內文排版 / Co Co
出版者 / 哈福企業有限公司
地址 / 新北市板橋區五權街 16 號
封面內文圖 / 取材自 Shutterstock

email ╱ welike8686@Gmail.com
電話╱（02）2808-4587
傳真╱（02）2808-6245
出版日期╱ 2020 年 10 月
台幣定價╱ 330 元
港幣定價╱ 110 元
Copyright © Harvard Enterprise Co., Ltd

總代理╱采舍國際有限公司
地址╱新北市中和區中山路二段 366 巷 10 號 3 樓
電話╱（02）8245-8786
傳真╱（02）8245-8718

Original Copyright © EDS Culture Co., Ltd.